"Stoney," She Protested, "I Think We Should Stop."

"I know you think we should," came the quick rejoinder, "but do you really want to?"

Kiki, powerless to respond, could only shake her head as their lips were again fused in a warm union. She knew better, but suddenly she didn't care at all. She only wanted Stoney's arms to stay around her forever, his lips to know every part of her, and she wanted to stop this foolish charade—she wanted to know every part of him as well. She breathed in the masculine scent of his cologne and forced herself not to think of the consequences. For once, she, who had made her living capturing special moments in photographs—for once, she too could afford to live one perfect moment.

SUZANNE MICHELLE

can't decide which she loves more—her family or writing. She lives in Texas and often writes about the West, which she knows so well. When she's not busy writing, she's often to be found with her nose in a book, because reading is another one of her favorite activities.

Dear Reader:

SILHOUETTE DESIRE is an exciting new line of contemporary romances from Silhouette Books. During the past year, many Silhouette readers have written in telling us what other types of stories they'd like to read from Silhouette, and we've kept these comments and suggestions in mind in developing SILHOUETTE DESIRE.

DESIREs feature all of the elements you like to see in a romance, plus a more sensual, provocative story. So if you want to experience all the excitement, passion and joy of falling in love, then SILHOUETTE DESIRE is for you.

I hope you enjoy this book and all the wonderful stories to come from SILHOUETTE DESIRE. I'd appreciate any thoughts you'd like to share with us on new SILHOUETTE DESIRE, and I invite you to write to us at the address below:

Karen Solem
Editor-in-Chief
Silhouette Books
P.O. Box 769
New York, N.Y. 10019

SUZANNE MICHELLE
Stormy Serenade

Silhouette Desire

Published by Silhouette Books New York
America's Publisher of Contemporary Romance

Other Silhouette Books by Suzanne Michelle

Enchanted Desert
Silver Promises
No Place for a Woman

SILHOUETTE BOOKS, a Division of Simon & Schuster, Inc.
1230 Avenue of the Americas, New York, N.Y. 10020

Copyright © 1983 by Suzanne Michelle

Distributed by Pocket Books

ISBN: 0-671-47114-7

First Silhouette Books printing July, 1983

10 9 8 7 6 5 4 3 2 1

America's Publisher of Contemporary Romance

Printed in the U.S.A.

Stormy
Serenade

1

The huge gleaming structure dominated the landscape as far as the eye could see, and the black sky
dotted with stars provided a dramatic backdrop. Kiki
Andrews carefully locked the rented car and stood
for a moment, marveling at the tremendous size of
the stadium. It seemed appropriate to her that the
newest singing sensation, Stoney Blue, should begin
his first major tour here at the Houston Rodeo at the
Astrodome. His first single, "On the Side of the
Angels," had swept the country—literally overnight
—three months ago, and Stoney Blue was a house-
hold word the next morning. She was glad to be
back in Texas, even if Stoney Blue was the reason.
Joining the crowd, she headed for the Dome.

Kiki shivered involuntarily from the cold night air
and silently wished that she liked country-western
music. As it was, she was afraid that her taste in

music would make this a difficult assignment. She had tried to convince her editor at *Lifestyle* magazine that there were other photographers who would be better suited for this particular assignment. She said she could personally give him the names of five good photographers who would jump at the chance to do an exclusive photo-essay of Stoney Blue for the magazine. But Sid Martin would have nothing to do with another photographer. "No!" he'd roared. "I want *you* to do this assignment. Blue's the hottest thing we've got. If you can't stand the music then wear earplugs, for Pete's sake." And no amount of persuasion, gentle or otherwise, would change his mind. And she had to admit to herself, however grudgingly, that there was a certain appeal to the fact that she would be returning to her own hometown as an internationally known and highly successful photographer, with exclusive rights to photograph everyone's dream man.

So she had thrown herself into the assignment, thinking that as long as she was going to do it, she might as well do it right. She read everything she could get her hands on about Stoney Blue and country music. Not that there was much out about the Texas singer, since his rise to fame had been so sudden and swift. He had grown up near Waco, the son of cotton farmers, and he was twenty-four years old. That she was getting in on this so early in the game was also appealing to Kiki, although she still couldn't say truthfully that she was completely looking forward to the job. For one thing, a young whiz-kid like Stoney Blue made her feel old at twenty-nine, and it was a feeling she was unaccustomed to.

After all, she thought ruefully to herself, twentynine's not ancient. Though she certainly had packed a lot into those twenty-nine years. After graduating with a degree in fine arts from the University of Houston, she had gone on to do graduate work, specializing in black and white photography. Then she had done freelance work for several noted magazines before taking a staff job at *Lifestyle*. The move to New York had come at a good time for her. Both of her parents had moved to Florida and Kiki had thought that she was through with Houston, through with Texas, ready to move on.

The job at *Lifestyle* had been good for her, she reflected. Sid had always made sure that she got the most interesting assignments, sending her all over the world in search of famous and infamous people whose lifestyles were of interest to the American magazine-buying public. Kiki had traveled with politicians, explorers, anthropologists, surfers, writers—the list went on and on. She had driven herself relentlessly, burying herself in her work, never stopping to get seriously involved with men. Oh, there had been a few brief relationships, but nothing special. She just hadn't had time. She was too busy making a name for herself. Sometimes, when she was between assignments, she was filled with an aching loneliness, an awareness that something was missing from her life. But she went right on to the next thing, quickly, trying not to think about it.

But here she was, back home again, face to face

with Houston one more time. She hesitated a moment, shifting the heavy leather bag that contained her cameras and equipment from one shoulder to the other, and was grateful that vanity hadn't been her only guide when she bought the suede leather jacket she was wearing. Fortunately, the soft leather was as warm as the fringe was appropriate for the occasion. With the leather bag secured on her shoulder, she continued the trek up the concrete ramp, and moments later, when she was standing in line at the gate, she found she was a little breathless.

Taking advantage of this momentary lull, she looked around at the crowd with great interest. The man next to her was smoking a pipe and had two little boys with him, both dressed up like cowboys with red hats and leather boots. They were pulling on him as if they could make the crowd move faster.

Kiki laughed good-naturedly at their boisterous persistence and asked the man about the crowd. "Is it always like this for the rodeo?" Her blue eyes were wide with disbelief as she looked up at him. He was considerably taller than her petite five foot, three inches.

"Oh, no, ma'am," he answered without hesitation in his polite Texas manner. "Not on your life. This is the first sellout we've had at the rodeo in a long time. But it's not the rodeo that's pulling them in, although there's always a good crowd for that, don't get me wrong. It's Stoney Blue. This town has gone crazy over that man. I've never seen anything like it. The paper says the Dome is sold out every night he's here. It's really amazing." He was shaking his head.

"Amazing may be an understatement," Kiki said ironically as they inched their way up the line.

"You from around here?" the man inquired with interest.

"Not anymore," she answered. "I used to be when I was growing up. Now I live in New York City."

"New York City. You don't say. You didn't come down here just for the rodeo, did you?" He looked at her in amazement.

"No, I'm a photographer. I'm here on assignment." Kiki was reluctant to give him the full details and was relieved to see they were the next in line.

"Hope you get some good pictures," he called over his shoulder as the little boys pulled him to the ticket taker.

"Yeah. Thanks. I hope so too," Kiki replied as she moved up in the line, and waved at him. Showing her press pass to the ticket taker, she stopped just long enough to ask directions to the press box.

"It's right up that elevator two floors. You can't miss it. The mezzanine on your left. Purple seats." The young man was dressed in red and gold and pointed in the direction of the escalator.

Kiki thanked him and headed in the direction he had indicated. Once on the escalator, she found that she had a perfect view of the crowd milling around below and she made a mental note to come back with her camera ready to take pictures. Never had she seen such glamorous western attire—silver belts and buckles and collar tips, silk shirts laden with intricate embroidery designs, expensive leather

11

boots in every imaginable shade. Sporty mink jackets and lots of heavy gold jewelry seemed to be the order of the day for many of the fashionably dressed women.

The myth of the lonesome cowboy in the Old West takes on an added dimension, she chuckled to herself, glad that she had purchased the suede jacket and worn a black string necktie with her tailored khaki pants and white silk shirt. The suede jacket and black string necktie were her only concession, however, to the western mood of the evening, though her soft leather boots couldn't have blended in more perfectly had she bought them especially for the occasion.

At the top of the escalator, she quite easily found the mezzanine, and a quick glance at her sporty aviator watch assured her that she still had a few minutes to powder her nose before she met Tully Jones, Stoney Blue's manager as well as drummer. She would be glad to have a few minutes to herself before she started work. After that, she knew it might be days before she had some time all to herself again. Kiki was a widely sought-after photographer, famous for intuitively capturing the essence of her subjects. She believed in immersing herself totally in the lives of the people she photographed. Despite her editor's notions to the contrary, she felt that the people and places around a person are important in knowing the whole person. This would be especially true with someone like Stoney Blue. Thinking back over her earlier conversation with the tall man in line, she hoped everyone here would be that friendly.

It'll make my job that much easier, she mused,

convinced that this audience was the key to Stoney Blue.

She found a ladies' room and ducked in just long enough to freshen her makeup. The plane had been two hours late and she had barely had time to check in at the Plaza Hotel, where she planned to stay during her visit to Houston. In her profession, she was used to living out of a suitcase, but the delay had made her feel more hurried than she liked to be.

Shaking herself from her reverie, she paused long enough to catch her breath and study her reflection in the mirror. Her short, naturally curly blond hair, her big blue eyes and her long lashes were the epitome of femininity. She had high cheekbones, flawless skin and a straight nose. She rarely wore much makeup—a hint of blue eye shadow, pale pink blusher, just a touch of mascara—and this evening was no exception to the rule. Once she was satisfied that she didn't look like she'd been on the run all day, she carefully blotted her lipstick and dabbed some of her favorite light floral perfume on her wrists and behind her ears. After she had run a brush through her soft honey-colored curls, she returned her makeup bag to the side pocket of her camera case where she kept her personal things. Slipping the leather strap over her shoulder, she took a deep breath and resolutely squared her shoulders.

This is it, she said to herself as she headed out the door. Time to get to work. So surely had her mind turned in the direction of her work that she was oblivious to the picture she made as she headed back to the mezzanine. Her cheeks were a flattering rose-pink from the cold air and brisk walk. Her honey-silk hair curled gently around her face, and her slender form moved quickly and easily with poise and self-assurance.

She had the amazing ability of the artist to shut out the rest of the world when she wanted to concentrate on her work. She had been footloose and fancy-free for most of her life, but when she turned her attention to her work, nothing would distract her. At times like that, she was a serious and gifted artist looking for just the right light if that's what she thought she needed—no detail was too meticulous, no chore too onerous. And right at that minute she was concentrating on Stoney Blue and his entourage. She wanted to get the truth on camera.

Pushing through the double glass doors, Kiki had to give her eyes a moment to adjust to the unexpected dimness of the plush bar and restaurant that fronted the seats for the press. Standing there looking around at her surroundings, she saw that the long narrow room was filled with tables and chairs and against one wall was a long mahogany bar with mirrors behind it.

While she was searching the room for a familiar face, she recognized a tall thin young man in a red flannel shirt who virtually vibrated with nervous energy as he constantly tugged at his neatly trimmed moustache. His dark black hair was parted down the middle and slicked back on both sides. Except for the red bandana tied around his neck and a pair of elaborately tooled cowboy boots, he looked like he sang in an old-fashioned barbershop quartet. Even if she hadn't recognized him from the few photographs she had seen of the band, she would have guessed that this young man played an important part in the group—his clothes were a dead giveaway.

"Hello," he said in a soft unassuming voice. "You must be Catherine Andrews."

"Yes, I am. But please call me Kiki. Everyone does." She extended her hand to clasp his larger one.

"That's right. I believe I did notice that in the portfolio Sid Martin sent us. He thinks a lot of you, you know. A whole lot!" Tully's voice was full of admiration and respect as he started guiding her to a table near the large glass windows that looked out over the rodeo grounds.

"Why, thank you. Thank you very much. Mostly I don't hear much from Sid unless something's wrong with my pictures, which isn't often. And he's not exactly a talker when it comes to praising his staff. You know, the strong silent type." She was keeping the conversation light, hoping to put Tully at ease. He seemed very nervous.

As they approached the table, Kiki got her first good look at the inside of the Astrodome. The rodeo parade was lining up, and the clowns were entertaining the crowd.

"I always forget how much I enjoy the rodeo until I see the clowns. Then it all comes back to me," she said to Tully as he pulled back a chair for her.

When he was sure she was comfortably seated, he sat down across from her. "That's right. You're originally from Houston, aren't you?" As if from longstanding habit, he pulled gently on his moustache, drumming the table with his other hand.

"Yes, I am, although it's been years since I lived

here. But"—she paused and looked directly at him, her blue eyes studying the situation—"we're not here to talk about me. It's you I'm interested in— Stoney Blue and everything that makes him what he is today. And I suspect that's going to be quite a mouthful, if his success is any indication." She stopped for a moment and took a quick sip of water, giving Tully a chance to speak.

"Well, that's what I'm here for. And I don't mind telling you right up front that I'm playing this by ear. This success story truly happened overnight and sometimes we get the feeling it has hold of us more than we have hold of it. So we're just learning the ropes in lots of ways. And Stoney's shy with the press. It took the whole band several days to get him to agree to let you come, and he wouldn't have agreed to it at all except you're the best in the country and he didn't see how he could say no." Tully took a gulp of his drink as if he had just unburdened himself from a heavy load.

"Hey, listen, don't worry. I'm used to people being shy. Everyone is shy with a photographer. But he'll get used to me soon enough. You just wait and see. In twenty-four hours, he won't even remember that I carry a camera. Say, what are you drinking?" she inquired in her straightforward, polite manner, hoping that she wouldn't hurt his feelings.

"Oh, gosh. I don't know what I'm thinking about. This is Coke—I've got to play tonight so this is all I allow myself," he explained. He leaned back in his chair and motioned to the waiter. "Would you like something to eat? You haven't had a chance to eat yet, have you?"

Kiki nodded her head yes, she would like something to eat. "I'm famished. It seems like forever since I had a sandwich on the plane." She gratefully took the menu the waiter offered her and quickly ordered a barbecue sandwich and a dark beer. "My mouth's been watering for barbecue ever since I learned I'd be coming to Texas," she explained to Tully as the waiter took her order. "Have you already eaten?" she asked Tully. He was nervously drumming on the table.

"No, I can't eat anything before a show," he explained somewhat sheepishly. "I guess we'll get used to this much success, but quite frankly, I'll be glad when tonight's over."

Kiki appreciated his openness and said sympathetically, "You know, you don't have to sit around here with me. I can take care of myself. If you have something you need to do, why don't you go on? We'll have plenty of time to talk later."

"Oh, no. I'm really glad to have something to do—it helps me to keep busy. I'm okay, really I am." He smiled reassuringly and tugged at his moustache again and looked out at the rodeo. "Look, the parade's starting."

With that, the two of them relaxed for the next few minutes and enjoyed the parade and the strikingly beautiful horses being ridden around the field. Kiki took advantage of the diversion to find out a little more about the drummer. He quite obviously admired Stoney Blue and it was soon apparent that he had a lot of faith in the other man's talent as well as a fondness for him personally. By the time the waiter brought Kiki's beer and sandwich, the two of them

17

were completely engrossed in their conversation, and Kiki found that she was beginning to be more and more interested in this singer everyone was raving about.

"Stonewall grew up in a little town near Waco. His parents knew he had a lot of talent but they wanted him to have a good education. They sent him to MIT where he got a degree in engineering."

"An engineer!" Kiki was genuinely astonished.

"Yes, and he graduated with honors," Tully said with pride. "Not that he'd ever tell you that. Anyway, while he liked MIT, he was always a little homesick for Texas. That's when he started writing songs in earnest—love songs and ballads mostly."

"Did you know him then?"

"Oh, yes, we were at MIT together. I was working my way through school in those days, playing drums, sometimes the piano, in a little bar near campus. One night Stoney came up and we started talking. We talked all night, the two of us. It was dawn before we went home. After that, Stoney came in regularly. Sometimes he played a new song on the piano and we'd fool around making up arrangements. Sometimes he'd sing. When he did that, a whole crowd would gather. After a while, the regulars began to ask for him and finally a couple of nights a week, Stoney would be there singing, playing the piano, sometimes a classical guitar. You know, he can play several instruments by ear, and all kinds of music. But the ones he did best were the songs he wrote himself, the soft country ballads about Texas. When he sang about Texas, he had a wistful quality about his voice, that sweetness that's making him so famous now. He puts his heart into it, you know, all the way. That's why he's so good. He's the genuine article." Tully stopped a moment, as if he had gone on too long, and drank the last of his Coke.

Kiki found that she was spellbound by his account and when she glanced at her watch, she was surprised to see how late it was.

"What time is the show?" she asked, concerned that she didn't keep Tully too long.

"We go on right after the steer roping," he explained. "That's about forty-five minutes from now. If you have everything you need, I think I'd better go join the group."

She laughed and said, "Please do. I don't want the drummer to be sitting around in the press box when the drums start to roll!"

Tully was laughing good-naturedly as he stood up from the table. "Oh, I almost forgot. There's a party later. Up in the Director's Club. Stoney's expecting you to join us there. He's looking forward to meeting you. So are the other guys."

"And I'm looking forward to meeting them," Kiki said with more enthusiasm than she would have thought possible a few hours ago. Tully told her how to find the Director's Club and they agreed to meet later.

"And listen. Thanks so much for everything. Really. You know, it's going to be okay. You guys are going to knock 'em dead. I can feel it in my bones." Kiki could tell by the look on his face that he was getting nervous again and she wanted to reassure him.

"Yeah, thanks a lot," he said gratefully, turning to

leave. "And I'm looking forward to working with you. It's been a pleasure meeting you." With that last remark, he turned and pushed through the glass doors and was gone.

Kiki thought he had meant what he said, and surprisingly enough, she was looking forward to working with him. There was a kind of openness in Tully that she found refreshing, unlike many of the rich and famous she had worked with. So far this group had managed to defy all the odds, she thought to herself as she began gathering up her things. Glancing at her watch, she saw that she still had about thirty minutes to spare. Tully's mood was contagious, she realized, and noting that she herself was restless and impatient, she decided to walk around the Astrodome.

When she returned to the press box, the steers were being corraled off the field and the clowns were finishing up their act. With professional expertise, she set up her camera and the long-range telephoto lens, settling herself comfortably in the plush purple seats. Her bird's-eye view of the crowd below was superb, but she knew that she'd have to get close to the stage to get her best shots. She exchanged cordial greetings with other photographers there, determined to relax and enjoy the show.

While she watched, a pickup truck pulled the big round stage out to the center of the field, and a crew of workmen dashed out to set up the instruments and test the microphones. When they finished, the lights went off and the huge stadium was plunged into darkness, except the brilliant spotlights trained on the main entrance where earlier the parade had started. An expectant hush fell over the crowd, and a few minutes later, the announcer's voice could be heard clearly and distinctly.

"Ladies and gentlemen, we are pleased to have with us tonight the latest sensation in country music, the young man whose recent release just hit the million mark and is still soaring. Ladies and gentlemen, here he is—Stoney Blue!"

From the moment Stoney Blue rode out on the back of a baby-blue Cadillac convertible to the moment he set foot on the stage, Kiki knew he was different from any man she had ever known. He was dressed simply, as she had expected, in blue jeans and a t-shirt and a tan suede jacket with fringe that hung down to his knees. His hair was pushed behind his ears and he wore tennis shoes instead of boots. His body was perfectly proportioned—tall with long muscular legs—and his t-shirt fit closely over his broad chest and wide shoulders. He was one man who didn't have to depend on clothes to enhance his looks because he was quite simply the most beautiful man she had ever seen. There was a delicate quality about him that somehow belied his height, and he was as graceful as he was handsome.

Kiki continued to study him through her telephoto lens. His dark blue eyes sparkled and when he smiled, his closely clipped moustache moved with his sensuous full lips. His full beard was short and neatly trimmed, giving him a distinguished look rarely seen on young men his age, and there was an eagerness about him that was irresistible. The way he stood once he was on stage—with his taut muscular legs slightly apart, his hands lovingly holding a guitar, a

faint smile on his face exuding masculine vitality—
gave new definition to the word charisma. While he
was waiting for the crowd to quiet down, he arched
an eyebrow and moved one leg slightly as he shifted
his weight and the crowd again went berserk.

Finally, when he started to sing, Kiki began to
understand why literally thousands of teenagers were
falling in the aisle. His soft clear voice had a plaintive
quality to it when he sang his own ballads, and Kiki,
in spite of herself, found that her whole body was
responding to the country-rock rhythm. Never had
she heard such a gravelly sexy voice.

After several songs, Kiki gave a start and looked at
her watch. The show was nearly half over and she
hadn't taken a single picture! With renewed vigor,
she threw herself into her work for the next several
minutes, photographing Stoney and the members of
his band and the audience, moving all around the
large press box getting just the right angle for each
shot. She was determined not to let herself be so
easily distracted again, and from then on she was all
business, following the music with only half her
attention and concentrating instead on the light and
shadows as they played across Stoney's face.

When the performance was over, the crowd asked
for more, and the giant scoreboard, repeating the
request, flashed MORE off and on across the screen.
As if he were unable to resist such a plea, Stoney
came back to the microphone for one more song.
This time he sang "On the Side of the Angels," the
song everyone had been waiting for, and he brought
the house down. Despite her good intentions, Kiki

found herself once again mesmerized by his performance. The sounds he made with his guitar were like a spell being thrown over the audience, and there could be no denying that he held the audience in the palm of his hand. When he finished, he made a sweeping bow and then ran quickly over to the waiting car. As he rode out of the stadium, he turned and waved, and several armed policemen had to run alongside the seats to keep the frantic crowd in check.

The lights were turned on again and the pickup truck pulled the stage off the field while the clowns began more tricks and tumbles. Kiki felt more than a little letdown and noticed that the rest of the crowd seemed subdued after nearly an hour of frenzy. Whatever his magic consisted of, Stoney Blue had completely won their hearts, Kiki mused as she began gathering up her equipment, and she had to admit that she too was one of the vanquished.

It took her nearly thirty minutes to wind things up in the press box and make her way through the crowds around the concession stands to the elevator that led to the Director's Club. She knew it was in one of the sky boxes high above the field. Taking the elevator up, she felt a thrill of anticipation that surprised her. As she stepped off the elevator, she saw several policemen holding back a gang of screaming teenage girls who were frantically trying to get past the guards into the club where Stoney must have been. Kiki pulled out her camera and took some quick shots, pleased that she had come upon the scene when she did. The police soon had control over the crowd, and Kiki, putting away her camera, was wondering how she was going to convince the police that she had been invited. Moments later, to her relief, Tully stepped out of another room, said something to one of the policemen, smiled and waved her over.

"Boy am I glad to see you," she said with relief to Tully. "I was beginning to wonder if I would ever see you again, much less get in this club!"

"Hey, you didn't think I'd forget you even for a minute, did you?" Tully grinned down at her. He seemed considerably more relaxed now, though his face was flushed and he was dripping with sweat. "I'm sorry I didn't give you a pass," he added with real regret. "What did you think of the show?"

Kiki was pleased that he seemed really interested in her opinion, and she answered without hesitation. "You all were sensational. Absolutely sensational. And you don't know what that means coming from me," she said, chuckling a little to herself.

"I don't understand," Tully asked, a puzzled look on his face.

"It's a long story. I'll tell you about it some other time. Come on, let's get something to drink." She put her arm through his and he guided her through the crowded room to one of the bars.

"A beer for the lady," he said, getting one for himself too. The room was packed with fans and well-wishers, all of whom wanted to get close to Stoney, and conversation was virtually impossible. Kiki and Tully were soon separated, and Kiki stood back, sipping the delicious ice-cold beer. A few minutes later, she saw Tully standing with Stoney on the other side of the room. Stoney glanced up and, listening to Tully, looked in Kiki's direction.

For one whirling moment that seemed to last for an eternity, Stoney Blue and Kiki Andrews stared at each other, neither one able to blink, much less look away. Feeling tremors of excitement course through her slender body, Kiki met his eyes for as long as she dared, and when she finally looked away, she felt as if he had touched the very depths of her soul, leaving her naked and vulnerable. No one had ever looked at her that way. When she looked up again, the moment was gone. Someone was shaking Stoney's hand, introducing himself and the others with him. While she watched, Stoney looked over at her again, winking this time when he caught her eye.

This was the shy man that Tully had warned her about? She could scarcely believe the intensity of that first look. It had happened so quickly that she would have doubted it completely if her legs hadn't felt as if they were going to give way any moment. She was relieved that she and Stoney were separated by so many people because she needed to catch her breath and collect her thoughts before she got much closer to this man who left her feeling so helpless. He was no doubt accustomed to having women fall head over heels in love with him.

Well, she had absolutely no intention of letting herself become emotionally involved with this man! This is one woman who plans to keep her head, she mused with determination, though she had an idea how easy it would be to succumb to his charms. But she was a professional photographer, *not* a groupie, and she had a job to do. She certainly didn't get to the top of her field by falling in love with every man who looked twice at her. Besides, Stoney Blue was just a kid.

She glanced surreptitiously at him as she finished her drink, and was once again dazzled by his incredible good looks. He made everyone else in the room dim by comparison. Suddenly it was important to her that she get a good night's rest. She wanted to be fresh the next morning and in top shape—because she had a feeling that she was going to have her hands full.

Surveying the room for Tully, she saw him surrounded by admirers and decided she would call him first thing in the morning and make her apologies. Right that minute she wanted nothing more than to be by herself, away from this crush of people. Quietly, she slipped out unnoticed. A few minutes later, as she walked out of the Astrodome and headed for the parking lot, the cold night air met her and she felt herself returning to reality. She had a job to do and she was determined that nothing get in her way—and that included her own feelings.

2

As she walked down the long corridor of the Warwick Hotel, Kiki marveled at the luxurious thickness of the plush carpet. She couldn't resist stopping in front of one of the elegant, ornate mirrors to make one last appraisal of her appearance. Her pert blue eyes showed no sign of the fatigue she might have expected after the long day she had put in yesterday, and what little makeup she wore was expertly applied so that her porcelain skin was enhanced by the pale blue eye shadow and natural pink lipstick. She had brushed her honey-silk hair until it curled freely in a flattering array of feminine softness.

She had taken special care in choosing her dress that morning, deciding on a sophisticated white tuxedo shirt to wear with tailored khaki pants and her favorite navy-blue velvet blazer. From long experience she knew that the people she photographed would be at ease if she herself were, and she was most relaxed when she was confident of her own appearance. In spite of her resolve to get a good night's sleep, she had spent a restless night going over in her memory every detail of the evening, from the moment Stoney Blue rode out on the field, waving to a wildly enthusiastic crowd, to that last exciting encore. He had held the crowd in the palm of his hand and she experienced that same powerless but intoxicating feeling later that evening when he had looked at her. At that moment he could have done anything he wanted with her.

Well, she thought to herself, that was no doubt what he expected. A man with that kind of charisma and talent must be used to getting his way. She had to be wary of that if she wanted to retain her professional distance. Nevertheless, she had to admit to herself that not only did she find the singer remarkably handsome, but somehow she was powerfully drawn to him.

Rousing herself from her reverie, she walked down the hall to Suite 316. As she stood outside his door, Kiki felt a thrill of anticipation as she took a deep breath and knocked. It was now or never, she thought to herself. After all, Stoney Blue wasn't the first celebrity she had worked with, and he wouldn't be the last. Expecting the door to open, she was completely taken aback when a dog started barking ferociously. With dismay, she checked the directions Tully had given her. Sure enough, 316 was the room number, clear as day.

Surely there must be some mistake, Kiki said to herself, pausing just a moment longer trying to decide what to do next. The dog was getting louder and more frantic by the minute and Kiki was afraid someone would come out of one of the other rooms to complain.

Just as she was turning to leave, she heard a muffled voice on the other side of the door. The dog's barking stopped and the door was opened just a crack. Kiki involuntarily moved back a step when she heard a groan. Then the door swung open completely and she was once again face to face with Stoney Blue. This time, however, he was clad only in a large towel tied around his waist.

"I must be dreaming. Tell me it's not a dream." The handsome singer was sleepily rubbing his eyes, apparently oblivious to his near-nakedness. "Beautiful blondes never knock on my door except when I'm dreaming." His tall muscular body fairly rippled with contentment as he stretched lazily.

In spite of herself, Kiki felt the powerful pull she had experienced the night before and she had to catch her breath at her immediate physical response to his closeness. Trying to keep the situation on a course she could control, she said with a lighthearted laugh, "If what I saw last night was any indication, then I'd say that's something of an exaggeration." The sound of her own voice restored her sense of propriety and she turned to go. "Maybe I should come back later. I seem to have caught you at a bad moment."

"I don't know about that," he said in his sexy, gravelly voice, his eyes beginning to be very alert as he looked her up and down, quite obviously approving of what he saw. "It's got all the makings of an extraordinarily good moment, I'd say. I just need a few more minutes to wake up. You're Kiki Andrews, aren't you? Tully pointed you out to me last night."

Something in his tone of voice referred to that moment the night before when they'd seen each other for the first time, but Kiki chose not to pick up on it. Instead she said with mock formality, "Stoney Blue, I presume."

At that Stoney broke into laughter, and his mood was so ingenuous that soon she was laughing with him. The ice broken, he invited her into the spacious living room, managing to be quite gracious in spite of the peculiar circumstances. Almost immediately, the large shaggy dog started licking Kiki's ankles in a play for attention.

"Oh, I forgot to introduce you to Waco. Waco, this is Kiki Andrews, a famous photographer. If you're a good dog, maybe she'll take your picture too. Come on, leave her alone. She didn't come to play with you." He pulled on the dog's collar, holding him back as Kiki came into the room, but as soon as Stoney let go, the friendly dog bounded over in Kiki's direction.

Kiki was not to be undone by Stoney's nonchalance. If he showed no sign of modesty, she certainly wasn't going to dredge any up. Two could play this game, she thought to herself as she knelt down to shake hands with Waco. "Hello, Waco, I'm glad to meet you. So you'd like to have your picture taken, would you? Well, I'll just have to see what we can do about that." The mutt had apparently taken a real liking to Kiki, for he kept licking her hand and nosing his head under her hand for more attention.

"Well, I must say he has good taste," Stoney said appreciatively as he picked up the telephone. "Sit down, won't you," he said, motioning toward a large, luxurious sofa. "I'll just order some coffee and then I believe I'd better slip into something a little less comfortable." He grinned over at her with unabashed pleasure, then walked into the bedroom to change.

While she was waiting Kiki played with Waco, a most rambunctious animal who wouldn't take no for an answer. "How on earth did you get this dog in the Warwick?" she asked as she rubbed Waco playfully. The large dog had rolled happily over on his back.

"Well, it took some effort," Stoney called through the open bedroom door. "Finally, Tully agreed to rent all the adjoining rooms and put up a big deposit. It's one of the few advantages I've discovered of having everyone in the world know who you are. Waco goes everywhere with me—my own security blanket."

Wondering what kind of grown man would admit to needing a security blanket, Kiki glanced around the hotel room, puzzled to see what she could learn about his personality, but Waco's affectionate attention kept her firmly in her seat. The dog was simply not going to let her get up and wander around.

Oh, well, Kiki thought to herself. At least I know who this man's best friend is. Laughing, she took a quick picture of Waco.

Stoney returned a few minutes later, clad in jeans and a startling blue t-shirt, emblazoned with the words "No place else but Texas." His long elegant feet were bare, and Kiki couldn't help being aware of how well the jeans were cut, molding his powerful thighs, and how strong his tanned arms looked next to the shirt's clinging short sleeves. But before he could say a word, there was a knock at the door, and Kiki's questions had to be temporarily put aside as room service arrived with coffee and a lovely continental breakfast.

They went outside to the terrace and sat at a table. In the best Houston tradition, the hard freeze of the night before couldn't withstand the light of day, and spring seemed to be in the air.

As he poured the coffee, Stoney said candidly, "I apologize for oversleeping this morning. I'm usually punctual to a fault. But the party last night wasn't over until late, and I had a hard time getting away. I should be coming to life with this cup of coffee, so if you want to start asking questions, go ahead. I can only say that the answers will probably get better as I wake up, so don't get discouraged at the beginning."

Kiki laughed and looked down at the few notes she had made in preparation for this interview. She had been prepared to like this man, but not to feel so overwhelmingly drawn to him. And seen up close, he was even more attractive than she had thought. Photographing him would be pure pleasure.

"Maybe I should tell you a little bit about the way I work. What I try to do is to really get to know the people I photograph, so that a single picture can illuminate a whole number of aspects about a person. I've done several other photo-essays like this one for *Lifestyle*. . . ."

"I'm familiar with your work," Stoney said, "and I know you're good, otherwise you wouldn't be here.

I don't like having my picture taken in the first place, but Tully is convinced that this kind of publicity is good for the band right now, so I told him if he had to do this to get me the best possible person. I didn't say the prettiest, but it looks like he came through on that count too."

Kiki blushed, thinking that maybe this was going to be harder than she had thought. "Why, thank you." Before he could say anything else, she went on, "What I'd like to do today, depending on the time you have, is to start taking some pictures this morning, right here, and then perhaps we could go outside and walk around—maybe through the park." She gestured at the green expanse of Hermann Park, just across the street from the Warwick.

"Sounds good to me," Stoney said affably. "Fire away." With those formalities out of the way, he seemed to relax considerably. Underneath his light-hearted banter, Kiki had rightly assumed that he was a little uneasy.

For the rest of the morning, she followed him around the hotel suite as he answered the phone, talked with other band members who dropped by to say good morning, and clowned around with Waco. Though it didn't have the format of a formal interview, Kiki felt that she was learning a lot about this man, but there was still something mysterious about him that she couldn't quite capture. Little bits of his life history tumbled out between pictures as she plied him with questions. Stonewall Blue was his real name, not a stage name, she discovered.

"I was working as a civil engineer," he told her as he stretched out lazily on the floor. He seemed to have completely forgotten the presence of the camera. "We had been playing small clubs around Austin, but when 'Angels' took off, we decided to go for broke."

Later in the morning he admitted, "This is a dangerous business. I mean, too much success too fast is a little dangerous. So I made sure that the first thing I did was to pay off the mortgage on my parents' farm, and then I started looking around the Hill Country for a little place of my own. So if the bottom should fall out tomorrow, at least I still have my home, and I could always go back to being an engineer." He was looking out the window at the busy street below.

Kiki had to admire his foresight, but she was hard-pressed to imagine Stoney Blue trapped in an office. He seemed too wild, too free. As it was, his pacing about the relatively small hotel rooms was beginning to remind Kiki of a caged animal, and she suggested that they go to the park.

"Now that sounds like a woman after my own heart," he said, moving in her direction. "Can you tell I'm beginning to feel a little cooped up in this hotel? Even if I am with the prettiest photographer in the country!"

There was an unexpected tenderness in his voice, and as Kiki looked up in surprise, he took the camera away from her and put his arms around her waist. She knew that he was going to kiss her—she had known all morning that this moment would arrive—and now that it was here, she was afraid of it. But all she could do was respond lamely, "I'd like to get some outdoor shots while the light's still good."

Stoney, however, was not to be diverted, and his lips were tender as he gently pressed them against hers. What began as a close embrace soon engulfed them in a rising tide of passion. His tongue crept through her barely parted lips, gently probing, exploring the tender recesses of the sweetness within. Kiki was all too aware of the sheer animal magnetism of the man, and when the kiss deepened, she could only moan with pleasure.

"I've wanted to do that from the moment I first saw you last night," Stoney whispered huskily. As she made a feeble attempt at moving away, he added, "And you wanted it too. I saw it in your eyes." Before she could reply, his lips claimed hers again and the only thing that mattered was the thrill she felt at Stoney's touch and the insistent desire that coursed through her body despite her good sense. She knew he was right.

From the moment she had first seen him, she felt that there was some kind of powerful magic at work—that this singer, this cowboy, this incredibly virile man was going to be someone special to her. As he teased her with the rough texture of his beard, Kiki reflected that it was like being held close to a bear—gentle for the moment, but one who could become dangerous at the slightest provocation. Already she could feel her nipples harden as she felt herself held against him and she knew that he was feeling the same powerful urges that she was.

Finally, Stoney drew back and looked down at her with desire and affection, a curious mingling of naked need and curiosity in his eyes. "I think," he said finally, "that there's more here than meets the eye."

"There always is," Kiki said lightly, desperately trying to regain her composure. "And now that we've done that, let's go to the park." With all the strength she could muster, she moved away from him, hoping her voice sounded more casual than she felt.

He laughed and said, "I know. You want to get some good outdoor shots." Good-naturedly, he went to the phone to order a picnic lunch from the hotel kitchen.

A few minutes later, they were walking out the door with a picnic basket, like so many other people seemed to be doing on this fine clear day. Waco was especially delighted to be outdoors, though not particularly enthusiastic about the leash Stoney had insisted upon. First they walked around the Mecom Fountain, immediately across the street from the Warwick, and Kiki got some good shots of Stoney and Waco with the water spraying behind them.

"So tell me, Stoney," Kiki asked as they entered the wooded park. "What do you like most about your life right now?" Being close to him was so comfortable and natural that she had to remind herself she was working, and she hoped the questions didn't sound too forced.

To her relief, Stoney considered the question seriously before answering. "Truthfully," he said slowly, "I'd have to say that I like the freedom. I mean I like doing what I do and getting paid for it. I liked being an engineer too, but I felt trapped. So far I really like the life on the road—I like working with my friends in the band; have a lot of respect for them—and mostly I like getting to meet different types of people. It seems almost sinful to get paid for making music—when that's the thing I like best in life!" For a moment his face looked terribly young, as if he could not believe his own good fortune.

Later, when they shared the picnic lunch packed by the hotel—delicious fruits and salads of every conceivable kind and a chilled bottle of dry white wine—they began to talk as if they were old friends. Stoney seemed genuinely interested in her work, asking her well-considered questions about the places she had been and the people she had worked with. She found herself responding to his open warmth, telling him things about herself she hadn't told anyone—or at least not in a long time. Those blue eyes of his made it impossible to lie to him— they seemed to see right through the person he was talking to. Kiki couldn't get over the easiness of their time together, and when Stoney put his arm around her shoulders it seemed perfectly natural, though she found his closeness more disturbing than she would have cared to admit.

They spent a lovely afternoon, Kiki taking pictures all the while. She couldn't help noticing how courteous Stoney was to all the people who recognized him, signing autographs with grace and charm. Kiki knew she was dangerously drawn to him. And she was lucky—her camera gave her the perfect excuse to observe him closely. She liked what she saw, though her cheeks flamed at the memory of that earlier kiss.

When a lovely redhead came up to Stoney, he allowed her to plant a kiss on his cheek. Kiki took a picture of that moment, gritting her teeth all the while, though she knew it was irrational to feel such jealousy. How could she feel so involved with a man she'd only known for less than twenty-four hours? A man she was likely to know for only a few more days at the most? It was absolutely senseless!

Stoney probed her gently as they walked along, asking her questions about her life in New York, her friends there, whether or not she ever missed Texas. "Oh, I do," she admitted, surprising even herself. "Today I feel like I could really come back here. But until I'm truly established, New York is the place for me. All the contacts are there. But I'm glad when my work gives me a chance to travel—I like seeing all the places I've seen. Sometimes I think I'd like my life to go on and on like this forever—new people, new places, always learning."

"I think it does go on forever," Stoney said quietly, "as long as you're young at heart." He seemed to be thoughtfully considering this.

Once again, Kiki was acutely aware of their five-year age difference—did he really think that she was so old that she had to worry about being young at heart? She was only twenty-nine! But she answered easily. "I think you're right," she agreed, "but I've never worried about growing old. My work keeps me young."

"That's all right, as long as you don't become a slave to it," Stoney stated with firmness in his voice. They were approaching the gates of the park and, as he talked, Stoney stopped and bought a red helium-filled balloon and handed it to Kiki. "But I really don't think you have to worry about that. You don't look like you'd be a slave to anything." He looked down at her with obvious fondness, and Kiki thought for one perilous moment he was going to kiss her again, right there in front of the park.

Instead he said, "Come on, let's go ride the miniature train," changing the subject as if he had thought better of it. "I'll race you." He looked down at Kiki and playfully pinched her nose.

Thirty minutes later, the two of them walked slowly through the park back to the hotel. Tully met them in the lobby, all business. "Get some good pictures? Great!" he said quickly, without even giving Kiki a chance to answer. "Now Stoney, it's time for rehearsal. See you tonight, Kiki," he said over his shoulder as he tried to hustle Stoney off.

"Now wait a minute," Stoney said firmly, removing Tully's hand from his arm. "I have a few things to say to Kiki and I'll be along in a second."

"Fine," Tully said, not noticing that he had irritated Stoney. "See you upstairs."

Stoney waited until Tully was out of earshot before beginning to speak. "I'm sorry about this, love," he said in a low voice, "but I guess I do have to go. They're really counting on me. But I'll see you at the Dome tonight. Right? Wait for me after the show."

Kiki nodded. She watched him until he disappeared into the elevator, giving him a short wave before turning to walk back to her own hotel, pulling on the string, giving the red balloon a bounce in the air. She had a lot to think about—it was just as well that she'd have some privacy to consider what had happened between the two of them.

After a quiet dinner at her hotel, Kiki decided to get over to the Astrodome a little early to avoid the terrible traffic and to take a look around the rodeo. She soon found herself caught up in the spirit of one of the largest rodeos in the world, and she was getting some great shots. The people were friendly and interesting, and it helped to take her mind off Stoney.

In the few hours that they'd been apart, she found that she'd been incapable of rational thought about him. Whenever she tried to tell herself that she was being foolish—that she was making too much out of what happened between them—she would find his image appearing before her eyes, and she would again feel the insistent pressure of his lips on hers—and she knew she was lost. She could only hope to get through the rest of this assignment without making a complete fool of herself. He was too young for her—she was five years older—she told herself reasonably. But no matter how logical she was, somehow she knew that Stoney was going to be more important to her than she cared to admit right now.

Kiki was brought back to reality when the lights in the Dome dimmed, signaling the beginning of the evening's entertainment. As a warmup group began to play, Kiki made her way backstage, hoping for and dreading her first glimpse of Stoney. She was grateful that the activity gave her a chance to observe him without his seeing her, and she watched the way he meticulously made preparations for the show, checking all of the equipment, offering praise or encouragement to the guys in the band and signing an occasional autograph. Kiki told herself, with no hesitation, that he's got what it takes to be a star. She felt a thrill of excitement run through her at the thought.

Just before he was to go on stage, Stoney spotted her, and he came over to give her a brief hug and kiss. Kiki found the contact arousing and tormenting in its brevity, but she was grateful for his touch. She knew that she hadn't been imagining the magic chemistry between them.

"Break a leg, cowboy," she said softly as he turned to walk toward the stage, and he shot her a quick grin, his white, even teeth gleaming in the darkness of his beard.

Throughout the show, Kiki found herself taking lots of pictures, not only of Stoney, but of the whole band as well as the fans who attempted to storm the stage. Stoney seemed a little nervous, but he soon settled into a smooth rendition of "On the Side of the Angels," and Kiki found herself gently singing along in a whisper. And to think I swore up and down I'd never like country music, she said to herself with a laugh. How people change!

But when that thought had a chance to really sink in, Kiki recoiled in horror. *People don't change overnight,* she reminded herself. Suddenly she felt the nervous tension of the day in every pore of her body. What could she be thinking of? How could she really think that she was changing so quickly? This was all happening much too fast. She knew that she was asking for trouble by even thinking of losing her heart to a man like Stoney. How could she have so little self-control? And what, after all, did she really know about him? Was she just another groupie? That thought struck terror in her heart, and as she watched him on the stage, crooning a tender country love song with softness and conviction, she also saw the expressions on the faces of the women in the first row of the audience.

Why, everybody must feel this way about him, she thought to herself. *I don't know what I could have been thinking.* Terrified to admit what she already knew, she determined to leave as soon as the band announced its last number. Too much had happened too fast. She was simply going to have to get this situation in focus, and that meant staying away from Stoney—at least for tonight, job or no job. So when the band launched into its last song, she turned and quickly made her way through the crowded Astrodome and out to the parking lot and back to the hotel. She was going to have a sleepless night, she could tell, but she knew that she needed time. A small voice inside her whispered—*You know what's going to happen. You know it's inevitable.*

3

The insistent knocking at the door seemed to be coming from far away and Kiki refused to admit that she was really hearing it. It was all simply a bad dream. Or, she thought as she struggled slowly to consciousness, it was room service with someone else's breakfast. "I didn't order anything!" she shouted at the closed door. "Go away!" After such a restless night, she thought she deserved what little extra sleep she could steal from the morning. "Go away!" she shouted again when the knocking continued.

Finally, when it became obvious that whoever was doing the knocking was *not* going to go away, she decided that the only way to stop the noise was to confront its maker. She struggled out of bed and went to the door, wearing only the comfortable man's shirt that she usually slept in. "All right, all right," she muttered as she fumbled with the lock before opening the door a crack. "What do you want?" She looked straight up into the eyes of Stoney Blue!

"Under the circumstances, I'd say that's a rather ill-advised question," he drawled, looking down at her with a smile, his dark blue eyes scanning her slender form. "You know," he continued in a slow deep tone, "we've got to stop meeting like this." Before she could make a move his lips claimed hers in a brief kiss. Kiki started to back away, but she was held captive by the warm pressure of his mouth, and she was briefly disappointed that the kiss did not linger and last.

"You may have a point there, cowboy," she said as she stepped back, clutching the front of her shirt together, for she had become uncomfortably aware of his eyes lingering on her exposed throat. "But come on in," she said, moving across the room. If he could have been so nonchalant yesterday, clad only in a towel, certainly she could show him that she wasn't fazed by being caught in her nightshirt. "What are you doing here, by the way?"

She opened the curtains to let the morning sunshine in and gazed down at busy Montrose Boulevard. She was trying to give herself some time to think, for it was all too obvious what Stoney would *like* to be doing here. He hadn't taken his eyes off her for a minute, and Kiki, while she was enjoying the situation just a little too much to be strictly professional, wondered how she was going to extricate herself from this awkward moment. She should make a point in the future, she told herself, of not being left alone with this man, especially in hotel rooms. They were simply too attracted to each other, that much was clear even now. And she was too tired of the short-term relationships that had characterized her haphazard love life. Besides, he was too young for her, she told herself again.

Temporarily lost in her own thoughts, she suddenly was brought back to the present by the touch of Stoney's warm hands on her shoulders as he turned her around to face him. "I came to see you," he said in a husky tone. "I was worried when you disappeared last night, and I wanted to be sure that you were okay; besides, I missed you. I thought maybe we could spend some time together today."

Kiki forced her eyes upward to meet his, hoping that she wouldn't reveal the inner turmoil she felt at being so close to him. But it was pointless; the attraction was simply too great. His strong arms firmly closed about her slender waist, drawing her next to him in a single fluid movement. As his arms went about her, she just surrendered, her mouth turning upward to meet him. As their lips touched, Kiki found herself caught up immediately in the warm current of passion that raced between them. His gentle, sensual kiss soon deepened into greedy exploration as his tongue probed the moist inner warmth of her mouth. Kiki let her arms go around his neck to draw him even closer, wanting the kiss to go on and on. She could feel the rough texture of his beard against her soft skin, and she reveled in the contrast of his warm mouth on hers.

Stoney lowered his mouth to her throat, teasing and tantalizing her. His sometimes gentle, sometimes nipping kisses almost drove her into a frenzy, and when he slipped one hand beneath her shirt to claim a satiny breast, she raised no objection, but rather moaned with the pleasure of it. Stoney's mouth crept lower, teasing her nipples with his lips, his hand gently cupping one breast while he kissed the other. Kiki could only rest against him, grateful for the strong arm that was still supporting her. She was not exactly a stranger to lovemaking, but this experience was evoking something entirely new in her. She had never felt this way before; she had never slipped into such a state of lazy sensual languor. Why, before she knew it, she'd be letting this boy do anything at all with her.

This boy! The very fact that the words had crossed her mind was enough to snap her out of it. What could she be thinking of? Not only was she supposed to photograph Stoney, but he was younger than she was! What was she letting herself get into? She struggled to free herself from his embrace, trying hard to ignore the fact that her body was completely aroused by his taste and touch. She had to put a stop to this now. When she quite firmly pressed against his chest, pushing him away, Stoney raised puzzled dark blue eyes to hers. "What's the matter?" he asked, his eyes searching hers. "Is something wrong?"

"What's wrong," said Kiki quickly, thinking that perhaps the best way to handle the situation would be to make light of it, hoping to avoid hurting his feelings. "What's wrong," she continued, "is that it's getting late and we need our breakfast. Aren't you still a growing boy?" She added this last in a teasing tone of voice, but she would have liked to have taken the words back as soon as she uttered them.

"I hope not," Stoney said quickly. "But I know what I'd like for breakfast." And his arms reached out for her.

"No, no," Kiki said, laughing and backing away. "Do me a favor though. Go downstairs to the restaurant and order the biggest breakfast they've got for me. I'll meet you there in fifteen minutes. All right?"

"We could have room service," Stoney began hopefully, but a glance at Kiki's face told him she had made up her mind. "All right," he said in a cool tone, turning to leave the room. "I'll meet you downstairs in fifteen minutes. But be on time—otherwise I'll deliver your breakfast here myself."

Kiki breathed a sigh of relief as the door closed behind him. I'm really going to have my hands full with this one, she told herself, though she knew that Stoney, the man, was not at all the problem. It was Kiki, the woman, not Kiki, the famous photographer, who was the problem. One second more in those arms of his and she might have— She shook her head, not wanting to acknowledge, even to herself, what she would have liked to have happened. Gathering up her clothes, she headed for a quick shower, a glance at the clock having warned her that she had already wasted five minutes. And she wouldn't put it past Stoney to arrive with her breakfast in hand at the appointed time. Somehow, some way, she was going to have to get through this assignment without getting too involved—if she wasn't already.

When Kiki descended to the restaurant on the street level of the hotel, she found Stoney seated at a table. Slipping into a chair opposite, she smiled her thanks as she reached for an elegant glass of what looked like orange juice, and took a deep gulp. When the bubbles tickled her nose, she began to sputter and Stoney began to laugh.

"What is this?" she gasped as she tried to catch her breath.

"It's a specialty of the house," he said reasonably. "They call it a Mimosa—orange juice and champagne. I thought surely you could handle your liquor better than that," he taunted as she gingerly took a second sip, finding the drink to be quite good.

"It is lovely," she agreed as she regained her composure. "It's just that it was such a surprise." With a hearty appetite, she turned to her food, a steaming platter of eggs Benedict.

"If I had my way," Stoney said, his voice unexpectedly serious, "every day would start with a lovely surprise. I thought that we were getting along just fine, Kiki, and then I just don't know what got into you."

"Oh, we were," Kiki agreed, her clear blue eyes wide and innocent. "It's just that I have a lot of work to do today and I need to get started, that's all." Silently she cursed herself for her dishonesty. She wished she had the courage to put an end to any hope he might have for a personal relationship right now. It wasn't fair to lead him on.

"Well, all right," Stoney consented in a reasonable tone. "Now how do you want to go about it? Where would you like to go?"

"What do you mean?" Kiki asked, and then she remembered with a jolt that she was, after all, supposed to be doing a photo-essay on this man. Right now she had focused all of her energy on finding some sort of reason to escape from his compelling presence. "Oh, no, Stoney," she said. "No more photographs today. I need to get into the darkroom and develop what I've already got so I can see how you're coming across for the photo-essay. Then I have to get the prints off to Sid Martin at *Lifestyle*."

"Well, I don't see any problem with that," Stoney said, leaning back in his chair, watching her gobble up the last bite of her breakfast. "I'm free all day. I'll just come along and watch. After all, *I'd* like to see how I'm coming across on film."

Kiki knew that the request seemed quite reasonable on the surface, but she also knew that she did her best work in the darkroom alone—and she couldn't quite bear the idea of being confined in such close quarters with this handsome man all afternoon. He already represented too much of a temptation as it was. "No way," she said blithely. "You see the photographs after they're developed—not during. Besides, just think of me as an artist in her studio. I need time and privacy for concentration. After all, you want me to make you look good, don't you?"

"Sure I do," Stoney agreed readily, but his blue eyes looked slightly disappointed. He pulled on his beard as if he were thinking of his next move. "But you're not getting off the hook so easily. If you're not going to spend the day with me, the very least thing you can do is to promise you'll have dinner with me tonight. Then you can show me those pictures. And then you can be my guest backstage at the rodeo tonight. I'm not letting you slip away again so easily. After all, I thought we were supposed to be working together on this."

To refuse him would be childish, Kiki thought to herself, and besides, she didn't have a good reason for turning him down. Even though everything suddenly seemed too complicated, she knew that she was somehow going to have to see this assignment through. "Okay, fine," she assented. "Where shall we meet?"

"Why don't you just come on over to the hotel room about seven?" Stoney asked. "Then we'll take it from there."

"Fine," said Kiki matter-of-factly, signing the check for breakfast and rising to go. "I'll see you then." She extended a slender hand for a handshake.

Stoney, in a surprisingly romantic gesture, took her proffered hand and raised it to his lips in a gentle kiss. As his lips grazed her fingertips, Kiki felt a thrill of sensual pleasure. Somehow he had a way of getting through to her, no matter what she did, no matter how businesslike she tried to be. This was going to be harder than she thought.

"See you tonight, pretty lady," he murmured in that gravelly voice of his, and then he was gone. Kiki stood there for a few minutes staring after him, then decided that the best remedy for this condition was work—and lots of it. After grabbing her equipment she headed for her rental car, deciding that she'd just stay in the darkroom until she had those pictures done. At least she would have a few hours to herself, without the overwhelming presence of Stoney Blue.

A few hours later, she told herself that she couldn't have been more wrong. If the man wasn't there to torment her in person, his image certainly was. She was surrounded by pictures of Stoney Blue—dozens of photos hung on the line to dry. Even the photos in the developing solution mocked her—suddenly, where there had been nothing but a blank sheet of paper, there would appear his handsome face, mocking her attempt to banish him from her thoughts.

He had to be one of the most fascinating men she had ever photographed, she admitted to herself, though he was proving himself to be one of the most elusive. She didn't seem to quite have him down yet. Something was missing in all the photographs. She had some great action shots of him singing with the band the first night of the rodeo, and some marvelous outdoor shots from the day at the park, but nothing that she thought really displayed the essence of the man—his contradictory gentleness and power, his shyness despite his success and his extraordinary ability to take a huge crowd and hold it in the palm of his hand while he made his music.

No, something's definitely missing here, Kiki told herself as she put the last photograph in the dryer and settled down to wait for it. I'll just have to keep on it. She couldn't help wondering if her attraction to the man was getting in the way of her professional ability, but she had had brief affairs occasionally with men she had photographed in the past, and somehow that didn't ring true to her. But then, she admonished herself ruefully, none of them had ever been deep-voiced country singers with dark beards that tickled during a kiss, and piercing blue eyes that seemed to see through a woman. Firmly resolved to come back to the present, she reminded herself that none of them had ever been that young, either.

She carefully packed the photos in a heavy mailer and dashed out to the airport to send them to Sid air freight. At least that way she would have some feedback from her editor sometime tomorrow. Besides, Stoney had only a short engagement at the rodeo. She was under pressure to finish this job and do it well, all within a limited time span.

Caught in Houston's fabled rush-hour traffic on the way back from the airport, Kiki found herself thinking ahead to the evening she would share with Stoney. Dinner sounded safe enough, and they would be surrounded by people at the rodeo. If she played her cards right, she could get some great shots of Stoney interacting with the audience and with the band. That way, at least there would always be a camera to place between them. As the traffic inched along, she couldn't help wishing that he wasn't just a little older, or even that they had met under different circumstances. But things are what they are, she told herself firmly as she pulled up in front of the Plaza and hurried in to dress. It was well after six o'clock by then and she wanted to be on time—to keep everything businesslike.

She emerged from the Plaza a few minutes later, and thinking that she would enjoy the soft night air of Houston, decided to walk to the Warwick. Winter seemed far away as she walked down the steps of the

Plaza and into the evening. She was all too conscious of the patrons of the sidewalk cafe across the street observing her progress and from the admiring glances of the men at the tables she knew that she looked good. Her shining golden curls responded well to Houston's humidity and framed her face becomingly. A hint of blue eye shadow brought out the color of her eyes, matching the filmy gauze shirt that was shot through with gold threads and which clung to her slender form gracefully. A gathered denim skirt fell gently to mid-calf, and her buttersoft suede leather boots completed her outfit, giving her a western look that she thought was quite appropriate for an evening at the rodeo.

She strode along the street purposefully, checking the pockets of her denim vest for the extra rolls of film that she always carried. Her camera bag seemed light and she found that she was looking forward to the evening ahead. Even though she hadn't been completely pleased with the initial photographs she'd taken of Stoney, she now faced the assignment as a challenge. If I can't do it, no one can, she told herself with determination as she knocked on the door of Stoney's hotel suite.

The door was suddenly opened with a flourish. "If Madame would care to enter?" said Stoney in an exaggerated French accent, grinning down at her. Kiki, unable to keep from laughing, walked through the open door to the hotel suite, which had virtually been transformed into a romantic French restaurant setting. Flowers were everywhere—and through the open terrace doors she could see an elegantly laid table for two, complete with flowers, candlelight and crystal wineglasses. A gorgeous buffet table was in readiness and champagne was cooling in a silver bucket. Stoney followed her through to the terrace. "Paris, Texas, it ain't," he said laughing. "Just wanted you to know that champagne at breakfast isn't the only surprise I have up my sleeve."

Kiki was so caught up in the magic of the moment that she could only return his laughing gaze, touched by the effort and concern on his part. "No, Paris, Texas, it ain't," she mimicked. "And thank you."

"No trouble at all." He smiled, his white teeth flashing. "No trouble at all."

Kiki was equally stunned by the sight of Stoney, who was ready for the evening's show at the rodeo. He was dressed all in black—tight-fitting jeans, an elegantly cut western shirt which molded his powerful chest and shiny black leather boots. Suddenly, he didn't look at all young, and she was aware of the sensual, animal magnetism of his presence. They were a man and a woman alone in an overwhelmingly romantic setting. Surely Stoney knew this, for he had obviously gone to some lengths to plan this dinner.

Kiki was pondering this as Stoney seated her at the table on the terrace. She remained silent while he ceremoniously poured her a glass of champagne from the bottle in the silver bucket, trying to think of an appropriate way to respond to all this preparation for what was obviously intended as a romantic overture. "To us—to tonight," Stoney said as he raised his glass in a toast, his black form starkly silhouetted against the rays of the setting sun.

Kiki sipped in silent acquiescence, not knowing

quite what to say. Finally, she mustered a feeble rejoinder, "But you've gone to so much trouble— this is so lovely."

"No trouble is too great when the lady is as pretty as you are," came the gallant reply. "And besides, you wouldn't see me all day so I had nothing to do with myself except cook up elaborate plans for this evening. That'll teach you." He laughed. "And how did those pictures come out anyway?"

"The photographs," Kiki responded, with a slight emphasis on the last word, "came out very well, thank you. I meant to bring them to show you, but somehow I seem to have left the copies in the hotel room. I sent them off to my editor today and I'm sure I'll hear from him sometime tomorrow. I like them, but I think I can do better. You are an intriguing subject, after all, but I don't think that I've quite captured you to my satisfaction." She stopped and flushed, suddenly realizing the meaning implicit in her last words.

"Believe me, Kiki," Stoney said in a tone dark with meaning, "if you really wanted to capture me, you wouldn't have any trouble at all. It'd be easier than a calf-roping contest."

"Well, the calf-roping contest never looked too easy to me," she joked, grateful for the straight line.

"I'm not like most cowboys—easy to get and hard to keep," Stoney said seriously. "If you want me, come and get me. I'll be waiting."

"What I want right now is some dinner," Kiki said, determined to change the subject as the air suddenly seemed charged with meaning. This young upstart was actually offering her a challenge—and one that would be hard to refuse at that. Somehow she had to defuse all the sexual energy that was floating around them. She bent her head to the plate of escargots that Stoney had brought her from the buffet. "This looks great," she said enthusiastically, skillfully removing one from its shell.

"I hope it is," Stoney said, his voice a shade cooler. "I learned to love good food when I was in Boston—and I still do. I hope you weren't expecting chili and beer?" He asked the question in an almost plaintive tone, as if he were afraid of disappointing her.

"No, not chili and beer," Kiki said quickly between bites. "Maybe chicken-fried steak?" This broke the tension between them and they settled down to enjoy their dinner.

Eating was truly a sensual pleasure, Kiki reflected as she daintily scraped the last bit of chocolate mousse from her crystal dish. And this dinner had certainly been a feast—from the escargots through the elegant snapper Pontchartrain with tomatoes vinaigrette and tiny buttered new potatoes. The chef at the Warwick had certainly earned Kiki's undying respect.

"Tell me about your life in New York," Stoney asked, with surprising intensity in his voice. "I've only visited there once, so I can't imagine living there."

"My life in New York," Kiki mused, hard-put to know where to begin. "To tell you the truth, I don't spend much time in New York itself except for the interim between assignments. It's like life in any other big city—busy, crazy, lonely." She was surprised at her own honesty in making this admission. Stoney gave her a sympathetic smile, the expression on his face urging her to continue. "I share a loft with a few other photographers, but we're hardly ever in town at the same time, and when we are, all we talk about is work. I have a few friends, of course, but I don't really have much time for them. I want to be the best photographer I can be, you see, and that doesn't leave much time for a social life. My entire life revolves around my work." She was amazed at how tired she sounded.

"I know what you mean," Stoney said quickly. "Sometimes I think that I'd go crazy if it weren't for the guys in the band. We all keep each other sane. I don't think I'd ever make it as a solo act."

"Oh, you would too," Kiki insisted, reaching forward to touch his hand. "You've got what it takes."

"Thanks." Stoney smiled, capturing her hand in his own. "But we've already spent hours talking about me. I want to know about you."

"All right," Kiki continued, trying to decide where to start. "I do miss Texas sometimes. It was home for me for a long time, but after my parents moved away I just fled to New York and buried myself in my work." She ignored his quick look of sympathy and went on. "Now that I'm back here, though, I remember what it was I always loved about Texas—the wide open spaces, the friendliness of the people, the spirit of adventure. But I'm afraid that my work keeps me in New York—at least as a home base. All my contacts are there."

"Sounds pretty bleak," Stoney commented, a

strange expression darkening his eyes. "Sure there isn't some special man who makes it all worth it?"

"No," Kiki insisted, "I told you. My work is my great love—but I like it that way." She couldn't help but notice that Stoney looked slightly relieved. For the first time, Kiki realized that her life *was* pretty bleak. Granted, she had a great many things that other people thought they wanted, but she had so few friends when it came right down to it. For some reason, she suddenly felt defensive, as if she'd exposed too much of herself, and she attempted to turn the conversation to a lighter subject.

They had finished dinner and were drinking coffee on the terrace, enjoying the view down Main Street. Kiki found herself breathing in the cool night air of Houston and admiring the citronella candles in their colorful glass containers, and she realized just how happy she was to be back in Houston after such a long absence. She was glad to have shared this evening with Stoney, glad that she had opened up to him. His thoughtfulness and perceptiveness were delightful.

As night closed in around them, they agreed to move into the sitting room with their coffee, and Kiki had become aware of an uncomfortable chill in the air. She gave a surreptitious glance at her watch, thinking that they should be leaving for the Astrodome soon. At any rate, Stoney had a show to do in an hour, so surely she would be safe with him until then. She would probably be safe with him—but would he be safe with her? She knew that during dinner she had had moments of true self-doubt, thinking that she should let herself enjoy this relationship. Stoney obviously was interested in her, and she knew that she wanted him, at least in a physical sense. The constant awareness of her age, however, made her a little nervous. Besides, she didn't want just another casual relationship. She had had too many of those already. But it was a shame.

She took a seat on the comfortable sofa and was relieved to see that Stoney, guitar in hand, seated himself in a chair opposite. "If you don't mind," he said politely, "I'd like to take a few moments and warm up. I've been working on a new song and I'd like to try it out."

Kiki nodded appreciatively and snuggled up in a corner of the sofa with her coffee, pleased that he would practice like this in front of her. She thought of taking out her camera for a few shots, but she was reluctant to break the spell that Stoney cast with his husky, low voice and the magic of his fingers on the guitar strings. He sang a soft version of "On the Side of the Angels" and Kiki realized that she could like this music—or at least certain bits of it. It *was*, after all, the music she had grown up with.

When Stoney finished the song, she broke into applause, and he quickly started strumming a gentle melody. When she raised a questioning eyebrow, he simply stated, "I don't have the words yet," and continued to the end of the melody. She was fascinated by the creative process at work, by the way he seemed to be putting the pieces of the melody together. She closed her eyes and rested her head against the back of the sofa, opening them only when the song was over and Stoney had moved across the room to seat himself next to her.

"So how did you like it?" he asked, a finger reaching out to trace the line of her high cheekbone. Kiki was so aware of the touch of his finger that she was almost unable to remember the question.

"I loved it," she said quickly, not wanting to betray how she felt herself falling under the thrill of his touch.

"Good," he said softly, "because the melody reminds me of you. I don't have a picture of the song in my mind yet"—he smiled at the irony of his words—"but I think I have the right feeling for it." And slowly, inexorably, he bent his head to hers, teasing her face with light tender butterfly kisses before he finally claimed her lips in a possessive deep kiss.

And Kiki, all earlier resolve flown, could only respond with all the passion that she knew was inherent in her nature. Oh, there had been men in her life before, but none of them had ever written a song for her. The romantic gesture touched her, but she sensed that it was more than a mere gesture— that it was something Stoney would only do with passion and conviction. She didn't need the words; she had the melody—and the thread of joy running through her body had nothing to do with anything except the music that Stoney could evoke with his lips and hands.

The kiss deepened and went on, and Kiki found her tongue inside his mouth; she rejoiced in the mingled sweetness she found there. She felt that his caress had the same power and urgency that his music did—and the sensual emotions that she found herself experiencing were new to her—in the same sense that she had never before heard this new and lovely music.

"My, you are a picture." Stoney laughed as he drew back to look at her. He laughed in husky tones and bent to trace the line of her throat with teasing kisses, his hand tracing the outline of a breast underneath the thin film of the gauze shirt. Kiki was warmed by his touch, yet at the same instant her first impulse was to put an end to this lovemaking. But it was simply so right, so delicious, that she could only succumb to his passionate exploration. When his hand moved to outline her thigh over the denim skirt, Kiki felt that she should call a halt to this. "Stoney," she protested, "I think we should stop."

"I know you think we should," came the quick rejoinder, "but do you really want to?"

Kiki, powerless to respond, could only shake her head as their lips were again fused in a warm union. She knew better, she told herself that she did, but suddenly she didn't care at all—she only wanted Stoney's arms to stay around her forever, she wanted his lips to know every part of her and she wanted to stop this foolish charade—she wanted to know every part of him as well. She breathed in the strong masculine scent of his cologne, and forced herself not to think of the consequences. For once, she, who had made her living capturing special moments in photographs—for once, she too could afford to live one perfect moment.

Stoney's fingers were busy at the buttons of her gauze shirt, and Kiki was proving an active accomplice in her own seduction—her fingers teasing the mass of dark hair which peeked from the throat of his shirt—when they were interrupted by a knock at the door and a low voice beyond it. "Meet you downstairs in five minutes, Stoney," came the unmistakable tones of Tully, acting in his capacity as manager.

Stoney muffled a curse against Kiki's throat as he lifted his head. "Right!" he called in hoarse tones. "Be right there."

"Later, love?" he said with a questioning glance as he reluctantly buttoned her blouse and stood to grab his guitar case. As she joined him at the door, she could only nod, conscious that she was making a promise she would have to keep, knowing with all her heart that it was a promise she wanted to make.

4

Kiki wasn't the only one mesmerized by Stoney Blue's performance that night, his last in the Astrodome. The standing-room-only crowd had quieted almost immediately when the lights were dimmed and the giant spotlights swung across the rodeo grounds to finally settle on the big round stage and Stoney Blue, sitting casually on one corner of the piano bench, his guitar across his knee, his fingers plucking a tune. When he had started singing, the crowd, restless only a few moments before, became quiet enough to hear a pin drop. It was as if he were casting a spell across the audience. The simplicity of his heartfelt ballads was a welcome relief from the mindless repetition of hard rock and disco and it was easy to understand why Stoney Blue's music was sweeping up all the charts—not just country-western.

Kiki had gone backstage with Stoney and the band, where she took some good pictures of them preparing for the show. Minutes before the evening's entertainment started, she had raced back up to the press box. She had taken some close-ups and she wanted to be sure she had equally good long-distance shots. When she was satisfied that she had covered every angle, she had settled back comfortably in the plush seat and given herself up to the magical spell that captivated so many. When the show was over, the crowd kept bringing Stoney back for encore after encore. If they had had their way, he would never have stopped singing. When it became apparent that he was finished, Kiki was as disappointed as the audience that he wasn't going to keep on singing for the rest of the night.

Kiki started gathering up her things, eager to join him backstage. She was caught up in the excitement of the moment—and she and Stoney would probably pick up where they had left off before the performance. She also knew that she would probably have to reckon with her actions the next day. But at that moment, she was giving little thought to the consequences. Right now, nothing mattered to her except that she find Stoney.

When she finally saw him backstage, she could tell by the look on his face that he had been waiting for her, and when she ran up to him, he held her briefly in his arms, his eyes probing hers intently for a moment.

"When you're away from me, I begin to think you're just a figment of my imagination—the beautiful blonde in a dream," he whispered huskily.

She felt his warm breath on her neck as he spoke and an electric thrill coursed through her body. "You feel real enough to me!" She stepped back so she could see him better and smiled.

"I *know* what I'm feeling right now is real," Stoney said with a grin, pushing a stray tendril of hair from her face. "So real that I think we'd better get out of here."

"I'm with you, cowboy," Kiki said with a dazzling smile. She hoped she sounded more nonchalant than she felt—her heart was racing and she knew it would be difficult to keep her capricious emotions in check for much longer.

Putting his arm possessively around her shoulders, Stoney guided her out to the luxurious Winnebago that the band fondly called The Bus. Tully and Ace, the bass guitarist, were flipping a coin to see who would drive. The redheaded Ace lost, and with a mock grumble of discontent, he got behind the wheel. Ramsey, who wore a patch over one eye, was rummaging around in the tiny but efficient kitchen, looking for something to eat. Waco was curled up asleep in one of the seats, and seemed completely unconcerned about the comings and goings of the band. When Stoney got in, Waco opened his eyes and wagged his tail half-heartedly and then went back to sleep.

"Fame and fortune sure haven't made much difference to Waco." Kiki laughed as she sat down next to him, rubbing him behind the ears.

"The only thing that dog would cross a street for is a t-bone steak," Ace called from his place at the front of The Bus. "He keeps us humble."

"A t-bone steak is about the only thing I'd cross a street for myself," Ramsey countered from the kitchen.

They all laughed at Ramsey, who had settled for a tuna sandwich left over from the day before. The band seemed to take Kiki's presence for granted and they joked and kidded with each other during the short ride back to the Warwick. Kiki enjoyed the closeness that was evident in the easy camaraderie and was pleased to be a part of it, although she began to have a sense of the very real human quality of those men who had seemed so magical on the stage. She and Stoney remained somewhat removed from the general banter. Stoney had scarcely taken his eyes off her, and even though Kiki began to sense that the spell was broken by their good-humored joking, she was still content to sit with her head resting against Stoney, his arm around her shoulders.

Ace stopped The Bus in front of the Warwick and handed the keys to the valet. Saying good night to Tully and Ace, who agreed to take Waco upstairs, Stoney said to Kiki, "Let's go get a drink. I need to unwind a bit."

Kiki was relieved that the other members of the band would go on without them. Now that the moment was upon them, she felt a sensation of panic and she was grateful to Stoney for suggesting a drink. She somehow wasn't ready to go straight up to the room, and the plush bar was filled with soft light and seemed an ideal place for them to relax. The waiter placed a bowl of mixed nuts on the table and Stoney ordered a bottle of dry white wine. After the waiter had taken their order, Kiki excused herself for a moment, and headed for the ladies' room.

Once alone in the elegant powder room, she looked at herself in the mirror—she was having second thoughts about the wisdom of going through with this evening. She was powerfully attracted to this man, but her professional sense told her that she had no business getting emotionally involved with him. And the fact that he was five years younger didn't help at all.

Studying her reflection in the mirror thoughtfully, she told herself that she was just asking for trouble. This was Stoney's last night in Houston. Tomorrow he and the band headed for Austin as they continued their tour—and she would be just another one-night stand. The reality of that hit her with full force and she knew she wanted nothing to do with it. I've got more sense than that, she told her reflection as she gave her hair a quick brush and touched up her makeup. At least she still looked fresh, and she was relieved that her outward demeanor gave no hint of the turmoil raging within her.

You're going to go out there and drink a glass of wine with him and say it's been fun. So long, cowboy—if you're ever in the Big Apple, look me up. After all, she had enough pictures now, and it was time she went back home. With that resolved, she joined Stoney at the table.

However, she had neglected to take into account the incredible charisma and charm of Stoney Blue— the man had absolutely no intention of letting her go so easily. When she returned to the dimly lit room, he was just pouring her a glass of wine.

"Ah, the lady of my dreams returns," he said lightly, handing her the glass.

"Did you think I wouldn't?" Kiki returned with false gaiety as she sat down, but she had trouble meeting his penetrating blue eyes. She knew there was nothing she could hide from him and she was afraid that he would see behind her mask of cheerfulness.

"To us," Stoney said, lifting his glass to hers. He smiled but his eyes were searching her face for something he apparently sensed.

"The show was wonderful," Kiki said quickly, hoping to change the subject.

But Stoney would have nothing to do with it. "What's wrong, Kiki?" he asked gently, placing his hand over hers tenderly.

"Well, it's been an interesting assignment, and I guess I'm sorry you're leaving tomorrow." Somehow she had to sidestep this evening. "It's not an unusual feeling in this business," she continued earnestly. "I do my best work when I'm closely involved with the people I photograph and then when we're through it's sometimes a hard bond to break."

"This is not one you have to break, Kiki," he said softly. "I thought you knew that."

"It *is* one I have to break, Stoney. Don't you see? It happens all the time to me. Strong emotional attachments in just a few days. This one has been particularly strong." She was still avoiding his eyes. "You and Tully and Ace and Ramsey are all fascinating people. It's not surprising that I would find myself involved, but that's as far as I can let it go." She hoped she could soften the blow.

"This is different and you know it," Stoney said with sudden authority, setting his glass down on the table and taking both her hands in his. "This isn't just any involvement. It's not like a hundred others you've had. This is special and you know it."

Kiki couldn't meet his eyes. She stared down at the wine swirling in her glass. Without looking up at him, she could feel his eyes studying her. Impulsively, she decided to be as frank as possible, and she said softly, "Yes, I know. It *is* different and it *is* special." With that remark she gained some courage and met his eyes directly. "But that's all the more reason to leave well enough alone. That way it stays special and no one gets hurt. Tomorrow you'll be leaving Houston and I'll be flying back to New York and it'll be just another one-night stand. I can't bear that."

Very tenderly, Stoney brought her hand to his lips and kissed it saying, "You'll never be a one-night stand as far as I'm concerned. *You* may feel that way tomorrow, but I won't," and his voice had an insistent quality that was quite genuine.

Kiki looked at him with certainty in her wide blue eyes, knowing that he meant every word for she was falling under his spell again, that special magic that somehow existed between the two of them. The combined effects of the delicious wine and the soothing atmosphere of the room lessened the hold her rational mind had on her heart, and reason and good sense were banished as Kiki looked across the table into Stoney's incredibly beautiful blue eyes. She knew in her heart that this relationship and this man were somehow very different from any she had ever known.

"Let's go upstairs," Stoney said softly, his husky voice leaving no room for doubt, his eyes never leaving hers.

Kiki didn't know what to say. She only knew that she wanted this man more than anything else in the world, and right that minute nothing else mattered. Hand in hand they rode the elevator up to the third floor and Stoney's spacious suite.

"I seem to have taken leave of my senses," Kiki said once inside the living room. Stoney had turned on the lights and was opening another bottle of wine in the tiny kitchenette. She walked out on the balcony and looked down at the scene below her. The Mecom Fountain lit up at night was a stunning sight.

"If that's true, then so have I," Stoney said, coming up behind her with two glasses. "You don't think this is something that happens to me all the time, do you?"

Kiki took a sip and looked at him thoughtfully. "I don't know. But I do know there are thousands of women who'd change places with me right this instant. I should think that would be very hard to resist."

"What do you mean, hard to resist?" Stoney teased her, breaking the mood with a husky laugh. "You thinking about changing places with someone?"

"That's not what I meant and you know it," Kiki

said, laughing. He was standing beside her now, looking down at the street, his arm around her waist. He appeared to be relaxing after the night's work and she was glad that he was able to slow down a little with her. She only hoped that she appeared more relaxed than she felt, for his very nearness was sending ripples of sensual awareness through her entire body.

"Yeah, I know it," he answered softly without looking at her. He seemed to be enchanted with the fountain and the shining water falling in pools. "A fountain's a wonderful thing, isn't it, with no purpose except to be beautiful. It's somehow very relaxing, isn't it?"

"Yes, it is. Do you think if we tried to throw a coin in it from here, we'd hit it?" she asked fancifully.

"I don't know. Why don't we try?" Stoney pulled out some change from his pocket and threw it as hard as he could toward the fountain. They could hear it hit the street below so they knew it hadn't gone in the water.

"Here, let me try it," Kiki said, taking a coin from his hand. She tossed it high in the air only to hear the coin hit the cement below. "Looks like we're both lousy pitchers," she said, laughing as she turned toward him.

"I don't care," Stoney said, taking her in his arms. "I've already had all my wishes answered." With that, he made it plain what those wishes were. His kiss was insistent and ardent as his mouth sought hers with a sense of urgency. Kiki gave herself up to the sensation of his mouth on hers, her lips parting eagerly for his teasing tongue. Putting her arms around his neck, she drew him closer, thrilling to the pressure of his body against hers. She was conscious of his strength, his gentleness, his need for her.

"I feel as if we were made for each other," Stoney whispered as his lips teased the sensitive flesh of her throat. His hands had slipped to her waist and his fingers were gently tugging her blouse out of the waistband of her skirt, seeking the satiny flesh beneath it as if he could not bear for there to be anything between them.

"I know. I feel the same way," Kiki breathed, tracing circles with her tongue around his ear, teasing him. She had given herself up to the moment, to Stoney's need for her, and even more important, her need for him. All of her doubts had miraculously vanished. With Stoney's arm around her and her head resting against his broad shoulder, they silently made their way into the bedroom.

As Stoney began undressing Kiki, any fears she might have had that she would be more experienced than he were quickly dispelled by his proficient grace and deft hands; hands that already seemed to know her body well.

Kiki gasped with pleasure as he quickly undid the tiny buttons of her gauzy shirt, tormented by the trail of kisses he left on her bare flesh. At the touch of his hands on her back, she arched forward, delighting in the texture of his soft shirt against her, but determined to remove it, not wanting any barriers between them. She reached for its fastenings eagerly, but Stoney stopped her.

"Oh, no you don't," he laughed. "I know you— you'll take too long." And with a few quick movements, he took off the shirt, flinging it across the room to join her blouse in the corner where he had tossed it only a moment before. He pushed her gently toward the bed until she could feel it against the back of her legs. "There you go," he said gently, and pushed her back slowly. Kiki tumbled into the bed gracefully, eager to see what he would do next.

Stoney slowly, gently, removed her boots, teasing the lengths of her slim calves with the soft leather. She was surprised at the expertise with which he removed her skirt. As he drew away from her for a moment, Kiki reached for a sheet to cover herself out of instinctive modesty, as well as for protection from the cool night air which was blowing in through the open window.

"Don't do that." Stoney's voice was softly commanding, and she did as he said. "I like to look at you."

Kiki relaxed against the softness of the sheets, shivering a bit but enjoying his visual approbation. She lolled against the soft pillows while Stoney stood up to remove his jeans, never once taking his eyes off her. She had never been so aroused at the sight of a man. But then, she told herself with a startling honesty, she had never wanted a man so much. She enjoyed seeing his strong body gleaming in the moonlight, and she was tingling with anticipation as he settled himself on the bed next to her.

"You're so beautiful without clothes," he teased as he put one arm around her, the other tracing the outline of her body from shoulder to hip. "I wonder why you bother to wear them at all."

Kiki sighed with pleasure. It all felt so right. "You're

a fine one to talk. You look pretty good without clothes yourself. Maybe we should run away and join a nudist colony."

"Mmmm. Maybe we should," Stoney murmured, "but I like it fine right here, right now." His fingers traced lazy circles around her breasts, now and then teasing her rosy nipples into hard little peaks. She was enjoying the ease and affection of this lovemaking, wondering why she had ever thought of resisting him.

"Right here, right now," he repeated as he kissed every inch of her.

"Right there," Kiki agreed softly. "Oh yes, again."

Soon all words were superfluous as their lovemaking began in earnest. Kiki could feel Stoney's lazily sensual exploration of her body deepen into an urgent demand, and she responded with a need of equal intensity for him. Moments seemed to last forever as Stoney caressed her, his hands and his mouth seeking still more of her flesh, all the while murmuring the endearments that Kiki longed to hear. Kiki could only cling to him, her entire body rising to meet his insistent probing, her back arched in anticipation.

With his entire length suspended above her, he paused and raised his eyes to meet hers, and she saw with pleasure the look of desperate desire on his face. His voice was husky as he whispered, "I can't wait any longer."

"Neither can I," Kiki said quickly, but she could tell he already knew that from the expression in his eyes. He had known her answer from the pulsating rhythms of her body reaching up toward his, ready for the culmination of their union. With a graceful movement, he joined his body with hers, and both of them gasped with pleasure after the suspenseful moment when their two bodies became one.

He skillfully moved within her, steadily arousing her until she cried out for the inevitable release. Stoney quickly followed her over the threshold, signaling his own moment of completion with a short, sharp intake of breath. They lay in each other's arms, wonderfully exhausted, until finally they fell asleep.

Later, when she woke after a sound, restful sleep, Kiki found Stoney looking down at her thoughtfully, and she said, "Hello, cowboy."

"Hello, gorgeous. How are you?" His eyes studied hers intently, almost as if he were afraid of the answer.

"I couldn't be better. Why, did you have any serious doubts?" Kiki was surprised to discover some traces of real concern on his face.

"Well, I don't know. After the first flush wore off I thought—maybe—" He seemed a little sheepish and his voice faltered.

"You thought I was going to regret it?" Kiki sat up in bed, pulling the sheet up around her. She couldn't believe what she was hearing and the look on her face was incredulous.

"Something like that," Stoney admitted, wrapping his arms around her and pulling her closer. "You're as hard to hold on to as a melody I can almost sing but can't quite hear. I never know for sure what your next move will be." He was playing gently with a golden curl that had fallen in her face, twisting it around his finger.

"Always keep 'em guessing, that's what my daddy used to say back home on the ranch." Her lilting voice drew out each syllable in a mock Southern accent, and she hoped she could dispel his doubts with a little humor. But when she looked up at his eyes, she saw that he was quite serious—and realized that he needed a serious answer. "Look at me, Stoney Blue. I've had a lot of reservations about falling so head over heels in love with you practically overnight, and I suspect it's not going to be sunshine and roses here on out—we've got a lot of trouble spots to smooth over, a lot of obstacles. But none of that means that I regret it. You mean a lot to me, more than I would have thought possible a few days ago, and that counts for something, doesn't it?"

Stoney smiled at last. "Of course it does. It counts for a whole lot." With that, he pulled her closer and his lips descended to hers in a heated kiss, his hungry tongue parting her eager lips, searching furiously for the sweet secrets of her mouth. This time their lovemaking was less fevered than the first time; the pace was a leisurely one as they each enjoyed their newfound knowledge of each other. Kiki was delighted to find that her aggressive caresses both pleased and aroused him and she somehow seemed to know what excited him.

For his part, he left not an inch of her slender body untouched and she was caught up in the tempest of ecstasy she found in his arms. The music they made that night was this time a familiar melody, filling her heart with tenderness for this tall, lanky man beside her. Kiki reveled in the sensual languor that surrounded their lovemaking. When he took possession of her, it was with certainty and gentleness, and she called out his name as she felt her body arch against his male length.

The stillness of the room lay all around them, and since neither of them was willing to break the spell of the moment, each collaborated with the silence, eyes locked in mutual tenderness. Kiki knew that she had lost her heart to this man and found with him a sensual yearning that would never be completely satisfied.

"I've never felt this way before," she whispered softly.

"Neither have I," Stoney answered, his hand tracing lazy circles on the soft flesh above her breasts. "This is a whole new ballgame for me. And it makes everything else in my life seem irrelevant."

"That's what scares me the most," Kiki said with a gentle shudder.

"What do you mean?" Stoney asked, putting his arms around her, snuggling her against him as he propped pillows behind his head.

"We've both got incredibly demanding careers that are important to us and that's not irrelevant. It's something we have to contend with whether we like it or not."

Stoney was silent for a few minutes, turning over what she said in his mind and pondering it. "It doesn't have to be that complicated," he finally said, rolling over on his side to look at her. "You're making it more difficult than it is."

"Oh, I am, am I?" Kiki asked with a laugh. "Show

me it's easy. First thing tomorrow morning, you're leaving for Austin and I'm flying back to New York City where my editor is breathlessly waiting for these photographs. That doesn't sound easy to me."

"You don't have to go back to New York," Stoney said quickly, as if the thought had never occurred to him. "Come with me and the band on the tour. You can mail the pictures back. They'll probably get there just as fast—"

Kiki had to stop him before he got any further. "That's just the very thing I can't do. Can you drop what you're doing and go with me back to New York?"

"Well, of course not, but that's different—"

"How's it different?" Kiki's voice was beginning to sound a little strained. "Is your career more important than mine?" She knew that she was being unreasonable in even asking the question, but she was upset that they were having this argument already.

"Of course not," Stoney persisted. "It's just that I've got dates, schedules, places to be, auditoriums reserved, tickets sold. I can't stand up all those people. I'd never sell another record."

Of course, Kiki knew that what he said made sense, but her pride in her work and herself made it impossible for her to back down. "You think I don't have places to go and people to see? Would you like for me to tell you what my next ten assignments are and who's waiting where for me? I can't just wave a magic wand and make all my commitments disappear." Somehow she had to make him understand that her work was just as important to her as his was to him, even though she feared she might be asserting herself at a tremendous cost. "And besides, I enjoy my work and take great pride in it. It's what I like to do."

Stoney seemed to realize how upset she was, but it was too late. "Now *I'm* beginning to feel like a one-night stand," he said ruefully, pulling her close to him again, his voice soft and placating. "Let's not fight. If this is the only night we have together for a while, let's not ruin it. Okay?"

Kiki looked at him thoughtfully for a moment, her silent blue eyes studying his face. "I don't want to fight with you. That's the last thing on earth I want to happen. But it's this sort of thing I fear will get us in the end."

Stoney kissed her gently on the lips. "Now don't you go worrying about that. I've got a sure-fire cure for the ups and downs of life's rocky and treacherous path," he said with a grin, his voice filled with mock sympathy as he got out of bed, turned on a lamp and walked across the room to get his guitar.

Kiki had to laugh at his good humor, and as much as she hated to admit it even to herself, she knew he had saved the day with his clowning around. As he settled himself comfortably on the bed, his guitar in his lap, Kiki leaned back against the soft support of the large pillows, her worries completely gone for the moment.

"I'll sing you to sleep," he said softly, "and before you know it, it will be a new day for us both." With that last remark, he began playing the beautiful and melodious ballads he was so famous for and as Kiki listened, she knew he was right. The next morning they could start all over. Somehow they'd work it out together.

Finally, Stoney returned to the melody he had played with the day before, the one with no words yet. "I always seem to come back to this when I'm with you," he said, looking intently in her wide blue eyes. "Somehow it reminds me of you." He continued to work with the tune and, as drowsy as she was, Kiki enjoyed seeing him try first one thing and then another.

Just as sleep was about to overtake her, she mumbled dreamily, "C'mon, Stoney. I don't want to fall asleep by myself."

Stoney quietly put down his guitar and turned off the lamp, and when he got into bed, he took her in his arms and held her close. As he made himself comfortable, he said suddenly, as if he had just had a great idea, "You know, I think I'll name that song 'Stormy Serenade.' I believe it fits. I have a strong hunch that's what we're headed for—for better or for worse—a stormy serenade."

Kiki smiled sleepily as she snuggled up against him, too drowsy to respond, and moments later they were asleep in each other's arms.

5

~~~~~~~~~~~~~~~~

The tantalizing aroma of fresh coffee drifted through the bedroom, and when Kiki awoke with a start in a strange bed, it took her a few moments to remember where she was and who she was with. The other side of the rumpled bed was empty, but just as she turned over to survey the room, Stoney came through the door, whistling and pushing a cart with breakfast on it. Seeing him with nothing on except a blue terrycloth robe tied loosely around his waist was enough to bring the whole night back to her in a flash. Shaking her head slightly to be certain she was truly awake, Kiki wasn't sure what to make of it all.

"Good morning, gorgeous," Stoney said, giving her a light kiss on the lips. The fragrant smell of his aftershave lotion let her know he'd been up a while, and the sound of his cheerful voice was reassuring.

The blue robe highlighted the dazzling blue of his eyes and, despite her uncertainty, she felt a thrill of excitement. This was, after all, no stranger.

"Morning, cowboy," she returned affectionately, sitting up in bed, holding the sheet around her. "I hope that's food," she said. "I'm starving. When was the last time we ate, anyway?" Kiki was relieved to see breakfast. At least that way she would have something to do while she tried to assess her feelings. Besides, she *was* hungry.

"Weeks ago," Stoney replied cheerfully as he began uncovering the dishes. He was obviously in a good mood. "At least it seems that way to me. I don't remember the last time we ate. But this ought to do the trick—scrambled eggs, ham, biscuits and strawberry jam, orange juice and coffee. Where would you like to start?"

Kiki crinkled her nose thoughtfully, as if she were having a hard time making up her mind. "Well, that depends . . . is the orange juice spiked this time?" she asked cautiously, with a look of mock solemnity on her face. She was beginning to feel more like herself, and having breakfast with Stoney couldn't have seemed more natural—even if she *was* sitting up in the middle of the bed with only a sheet wrapped around her!

Remembering the orange juice and champagne he had surprised her with a few days before, Stoney laughed good-naturedly. "Not this time—the o.j.'s on the rocks. I felt like having a down-home breakfast this morning. Hope you like it." He poured a glass of orange juice and handed it to her.

"Like it? I haven't had breakfast in bed

since . . ."—she paused thoughtfully—"since . . . maybe I've never had breakfast in bed, come to think of it. Thank you very much." Looking across the bed at Stoney's tall form sent a shiver of delight through her, and she was acutely aware of her nakedness beneath the sheet—which reminded her that she hadn't even brought so much as a tooth-brush with her the night before.

"I'd like to serve you breakfast in bed every morning," Stoney said, his clear blue eyes searching her face.

"C'mon Stoney, don't start that again this morn-ing. We've been all through that, if you'll recall. And it doesn't get us anywhere," Kiki said reproachfully, knowing where it would lead. "I've got a plane to catch this afternoon, remember? New York City, here I come!" she said with what she hoped was a good imitation of enthusiasm. She didn't want him to know that the thought of leaving him in such a few short hours made her heart sink. She could not have a cloud of gloom hanging over their last hours together.

"What time do you plan on leaving for Austin?" she asked casually.

Stoney had pulled an overstuffed armchair close to the bed and was sitting in it, his feet propped on the edge of the bed. "Tully says we've got to leave by two if we're going to make it to Austin in time for the first show. I wish you'd change your mind and come with me."

"Stoney—" Kiki's blue eyes flashed and her voice was full of warning.

"Okay, okay. I hear you. I'll change the subject."

His face was a little woebegone as he searched around the room, obviously looking for something else to talk about. "Hey, have you looked outside yet? It's a *beautiful* day," he said, his voice entirely too cheerful. "The weather report—"

"Stoney, surely we don't have to talk about the weather." Kiki was a little irritated at his glibness. He was making fun of her.

"So what do you want me to talk about?" Stoney's voice was impatient and he began pacing around the room while he talked. "Here we are just getting to really know each other and you won't even take a few days off from work to be with me. I just don't understand it. I really don't."

"I see that you don't," Kiki said petulantly, all patience gone for the moment. "Look, I'm already goofing off on the job. I'm supposed to call Sid by nine o'clock his time and look at me. I don't even have a toothbrush, much less something to put on. I don't know what I'm thinking about. I really don't. Do I look like a photographer to you? I surely don't feel like one at the moment." She leaned over to the end table beside the bed and grabbed her watch. "Oh no, it's nine-thirty! If I don't call Sid right this minute I may not be a photographer much longer. At least not a paid photographer." And as she spoke the words, she realized that she really did feel guilty about not checking in with Sid. She didn't have the slightest idea how Sid felt about the photographs of Stoney; she only hoped they'd be all right. Somehow, she had a nagging suspicion that they weren't quite up to her usual standards—that her professional vision of Stoney was somehow blurred by her attraction to the man. With a determined look on her face, she started to get out of bed, but Stoney stopped her.

"Don't move. Here it is. You won't lose a minute's time." Stoney handed her the phone from the bedside table. "See how easy it is when two people are working together?" He looked at her thoughtfully for a moment before his face broke out in a grin. "Shall I dial it for you?"

Kiki had to laugh—this man was simply outrageous. It was impossible for her to stay mad at Stoney for very long. He just wouldn't allow it. "No, thank you. I can do it myself," she said, her good humor returning. But when she started dialing the phone, she began laughing again helplessly, and had to stop.

"What's the matter?" Stoney said, a half-smile on his face. He wasn't at all sure what was happening.

"Well, you don't know Sid so you can't appreciate this the way I do. But when I think what Sid would say if he could see me now. . . ." She started laughing again. This time she had tears in her eyes. "It's a good thing a video screen's not included with a telephone." She was rubbing the tears away with the back of her hand while she tried to stop laughing. "This is not what he'd call professional, let me tell you."

"Well, it may not be professional," Stoney said, taking the phone out of her hand and hanging it up. "But I like the way you look sitting in the middle of my bed." He brushed a stray curl from her face, looking into her wide blue eyes, and said softly, "It's good to see you laughing again."

Kiki had managed to regain her composure and when his arm went around her, she realized that there was no way she could resist him, not with those big blue eyes or that gravelly voice. Not this morning! She was sunk and she knew it. "Oh, Stoney, it's good to be laughing again," she said softly, her finger gently tracing his mouth. "You know, you really are someone special."

Roughly pushing away the sheet that separated them, Stoney's strong hands spanned her tiny waist, and Kiki was helpless to resist. His lips descended on hers, his hungry tongue eagerly searching her warm mouth for the secrets he knew were there. When his tongue parted her lips, Kiki could taste the good flavors of coffee and orange juice, and she pulled back suddenly. "Are we going to spill something?" She lay very still, remembering the dishes that were scattered everywhere.

"I don't think so," he answered without releasing her. "Let's not look." And with that, he began showering her neck with tiny kisses as his hands reached for her breasts. At first his movements were tentative, but when his questing hands found her nipples already erect in expectation, his exploration took on a new dimension of urgency. Kiki's arms went around him quite naturally, and she momentarily forgot everything else as she surrendered to his touch.

But when his hand gently traced a path upward along her thighs, she realized that things were going farther than she had intended. And the thought of her editor waiting for her call brought her sharply back to her senses. She knew she had better bring this to a halt if she wanted to keep her job—and unless she called Sid *soon,* that job was questionable. Gathering together what resistance she still had, she said gently, "Stoney, if we don't stop this, I might not ever get out of bed."

"That's just what I'm hoping," Stoney murmured as he rained kisses across her stomach and moved his hand toward the soft mound below. "At least we speak the same language," he teased, his eyes searching her face.

Kiki knew that she should resist, but his sensitive touch aroused her almost to the breaking point, and she realized that her feelings were clearly visible. She felt her face relax into a sensual smile. Her body stiffened briefly, then relaxed at his touch: a physical reflection of her inner conflict. But her heart was her guide and she knew that there was no denying the need she felt for him—a need which was increasing by the minute as his tongue and fingers brought her to greater heights of arousal. Her slender hips moved in rhythm with his touch, and she reached for him, wanting to feel his entire body pressed against her.

Stoney withdrew for a moment, leaning on one elbow, watching the expression on her face as his free hand teased one of her breasts. Just when she thought she could no longer stand the delicious torment of the few inches which separated his body from hers, the phone on the bedside table interrupted them with a jarring ring. Stoney collapsed on the bed beside her.

"I can't believe it," he groaned, covering the noisy phone with a pillow. "I just can't believe it."

"Saved by the bell," Kiki said, though she too

turned over with regret, her hand moving gently up and down Stoney's back, tracing lazy circles over his powerful muscles.

"That's not what I call saved," Stoney sighed, finally sitting up and running his fingers through his hair. "Now who do you suppose that is this time of morning?" The phone had not stopped ringing.

"You make it sound like it's early. At ten o'clock, it could be anyone." She took the pillow off the phone and eyed it curiously as it rang again and again.

"*You* make it sound like we're the only ones in the world still in bed," Stoney said playfully, deliberately ignoring the phone. "Maybe it'll go away if I don't answer it."

Kiki couldn't stand to hear the phone ring one more time, so she picked up the receiver and handed it to Stoney. "It might be someone important."

"Not a chance. You're the only important person in my life," Stoney said, kissing her as he took the receiver.

"Hello, Tully. Yeah. Who else would it have been?" Stoney frowned at Kiki and shook his head as he watched her dash out of bed and into the bathroom while he talked.

She blew a mischievous kiss to him as she shut the bathroom door. "Spoilsport," he called after her with a grin. "No, Tully, not you. Forget it, okay?"

While she found an extra toothbrush, Kiki could hear Stoney's low voice talking to Tully, and she knew they were finalizing their travel plans. Despite her high spirits, she felt her heart sink as she realized they would be parting in only a few hours and she didn't even know when she'd see him again.

Brushing her hair briskly, she decided that a shower might help. Turning on the water, she tested it with her hand until she was sure it was warm enough.

Stepping into the steamy spray, Kiki pulled the curtain behind her. Almost immediately, the soothing water had its effect on her, and without realizing what she was doing, Kiki began to hum. In just a few minutes, she was surprised to hear Stoney's sexy voice joining hers as he came into the bathroom and opened the curtain. Abruptly, she stopped, but before she had a chance to say a word, Stoney had slipped out of his robe and stepped in beside her.

"What did you stop for?" he asked. He seemed genuinely surprised as he put his hands on her waist and drew her close to him.

Kiki's fingers moved through the mass of curly hair on his powerful chest and she enjoyed the feel of his skin against hers. But she blushed furiously. "I don't know," she said with a modest laugh. "Somehow it's a little embarrassing to be caught humming in the shower with the country's latest singing rage. All of a sudden, I'm self-conscious."

Gently, Stoney brought her face up to his and kissed her tenderly on the lips. The warm splashing water only made her hair curl more, and she could feel the blush on her cheeks. "I've never seen you blush," he said softly.

"Well, you know, I've got a few old-fashioned traits that surprise even me sometimes," she returned with a laugh. "What are you doing in my shower anyway?" she demanded with mock indignation.

"Why, I'm an ecologist at heart," he countered.

"Surely you've heard the old expression, 'Save water—shower with a friend'?" He began to caress her, his hands covering her body with scented lather.

"And I thought we were more than just friends," Kiki taunted him, but her laughter soon changed to gasps of delight as he continued to touch her, leaving a trail of soap bubbles across her sensitive skin.

She took the soap away from him and returned the favor, teasing him as she trailed her fingers through the thick hair on his chest and beard, now soft to her touch. "Oh, we *are*—" he exclaimed as he clutched the towel rod for support as her hands sought him out. "We *are* more than just friends." Kiki delighted in the results of her teasing, enjoying having him at her mercy for a change. She was surprised at her own audacity, and she felt a thrill of sensual confidence at her ability to arouse this man.

Their mutual teasing soon became deadly serious, and it was all too obvious that they would have to do something about it. They slid into each other gracefully, without a moment's awkwardness, as if they had been doing this every morning of their lives. Kiki couldn't help but reflect that this had been a morning of firsts for her—the first time she had had breakfast in bed, the first time she had made love in the shower. She felt as if she were a new and different person—as if Stoney were somehow changing her in some subtle and powerful way—and she liked it. She liked it just fine.

Moments later, Stoney said huskily, "I think I'm clean enough. How about you?"

"Let's go dry off," Kiki said, the erotic mood still enveloping her as she stepped out of the shower.

"Your wish is my command," Stoney said gallantly, holding open the shower curtain for her. He obviously was not eager to break the spell of the moment.

Within a few minutes, they had dried each other off with a large fluffy towel and were stretched out on the bed, Stoney in his robe, Kiki in one of the shirts she had found hanging on the back of the bathroom door. She had brushed her hair and put on some lipstick. But she was not feeling as relaxed as she looked. Her gaze kept falling on the telephone beside her. Her mind was already on the call she had to make.

"Sid's going to wonder what happened to me," she said, resolutely sitting up and putting her hand on the receiver. "It's now or never." Dialing the number, she turned and looked at Stoney. "You know, it's nearly noon. I may never live this down. I can just hear it now. Old reliable Kiki has flipped out. Over a singer, no less. That's what they're going to be saying." She was waiting for someone to answer the phone on the other end.

Finally, after a short wait, the main switchboard put her through to Sid. "Hello, Kiki Andrews reporting in, sir," she said brightly, hoping her voice was convincingly lighthearted.

But Sid was not to be so easily assuaged, Kiki was discovering. "No, no, I'm fine, really I am." She looked down at the floor as she paused, giving Sid a chance to talk. When she began to speak again, she looked over at Stoney and shrugged her shoulders helplessly, but she had regained her customary composure and her voice was strong and clear. "Hey look, Sid, I'm sorry. How was I supposed to know you'd try to call me? For Pete's sake, Sid, I'm twenty-nine years old and you're not my father. I'm sorry you were worried but . . . c'mon, Sid . . . you know I can't promise that! . . . Okay, that much I can promise. When I say I'll call you at nine o'clock, I'll call you at nine o'clock—not three hours later. . . . No, you're right, it's not too much to ask. It's a deal. Thanks for being concerned. Even if it wasn't necessary." She looked over at Stoney and grinned. *"Now.* Back to business. How about the pictures? Did you get them? Are we all set?"

Kiki was silent for a few minutes, and the expression on her face changed slowly as she listened, registering first surprise, then puzzlement, then complete dismay.

"What's the matter?" Stoney asked with genuine concern.

But Kiki just shook her head at him, putting her finger to his lips, signaling silence. "I don't understand it, Sid. I really don't. I know they weren't my best work. Yeah, don't worry. I understand. I'll keep working on it. No problem." A few minutes later, a much subdued Kiki hung up the phone.

"Hey, what happened? It can't be that bad, can it?" Stoney was worried now.

"It's that bad. It really is. Sid doesn't like the photographs. He doesn't like any of the new batch." Her high spirits had faded to a despondent gloom as she puzzled over the failure of her photographs.

"Maybe I'm a lousy subject. Did you think of that?" Stoney put his arm around her in a comforting gesture. At this point, it was obvious that he would say anything to cheer her up. Even Kiki, as distressed as she was, could see that much. And the last thing she wanted at that moment was his pity. Besides, she was letting Stoney down too.

"Don't be silly," she said impatiently, pacing the room, eyeing Stoney speculatively all the while. "I'm missing something about you, but I don't know what it is. I've never had this experience before. And I can tell you right now, I don't like it. I know that those pictures weren't really my best work, but I certainly thought they were adequate. And I don't like being merely adequate—I want to be the best. I know I can be."

"I know you can be too," Stoney said with conviction, "otherwise you wouldn't be here. Remember, I wouldn't let just anyone take my picture. You'll get some great shots, Kiki, I promise you that. Even if it means I have to pose for you around the clock."

Kiki had to laugh at the offer, even though she knew that Stoney was incredibly sincere. "It's not a matter of posing, Stoney. It's a matter of working with what's there. To do my job well, I have to see what is there for this photo-essay in every moment that I'm with you. And I think the problem is that I don't see the essay at all anymore—I only see you. I've completely lost any distance I might have had and that could ruin the whole project. Somehow I have to get myself back together—I have to get back on the track." Filled with sudden resolve, she hurriedly began gathering up her clothes. Heading for the bathroom to dress, she said firmly, "And I'm going to get right on it. Starting *now!*"

Stoney was quiet for just a moment, as if he were digesting this new piece of information. Suddenly, he was no longer able to contain his enthusiasm as he realized the full implication of her words. "Whooopppee!" he finally yelled, picking up a pillow and throwing it in the air. "A miracle . . . a real live twentieth-century miracle."

Kiki rushed to the door, wondering what the commotion was all about. She was astonished to see Stoney dancing about the room joyfully, holding the pillow against him like a partner. "What on earth—" But before she had a chance to finish her question, Stoney had thrown the pillow aside, scooped her up in his arms, leading her in a dance around the room. Kiki was caught up in his excitement. When he finally pulled her playfully to the bed, she too was laughing breathlessly.

"Don't you see? It's wonderful. How can you look so sad?" Stoney asked, kissing her on the lips.

"Stoney, you don't understand." Trying to regain her composure, Kiki pleaded with him to be serious for a minute. "Something's wrong, terribly wrong. This has never happened to me . . . not ever. And if I don't pull out of this—"

"But you will," he said confidently, kissing her again. "You will. And in the meantime, we'll be together."

Kiki had to admit to herself that the prospect was appealing to her. The last thing she wanted was to leave Stoney . . . but there was more to it than that. She couldn't kid herself. "It's not that easy, Stoney," she said finally, a little annoyed that he could so easily dismiss her professional problems. Deep in her heart, her greatest fear was that she was already too involved with Stoney to have the objective viewpoint so essential to the kind of work she was doing. And she knew she had to put some distance between the two of them—and soon.

"Don't you see?" she said, slowly sitting up on the edge of the bed. "I'm already too involved. I've broken every rule in the book and I'm paying for it. It's got to stop. I'm going with you and the band, but not as your lover. I'm a professional photographer and I've got to start acting like one—not like some lovesick groupie. That's all there is to it," she said with obvious determination, and, as if the subject were closed, she started pulling on her boots.

"You must be kidding," Stoney said in disbelief. "You can't just snap your fingers and say we aren't lovers. It doesn't work that way."

"It's got to work that way, Stoney. I have no other choice. My work is too important to me. I can't just sit by and watch it go down the drain. I can't and I won't." And even Kiki was a little surprised at the determination in her voice.

But Stoney was not to be so easily put aside. "It's not going to work, Kiki. You can't just tell your heart what to feel, and you're kidding yourself if you think you can." His voice was gentle but firm. He seemed to sense that there was no arguing with her at that moment but he couldn't resist one final word. "And I'm not going to be two inches from your side. I won't let you forget your heart."

Kiki was a little surprised by the resolve she heard in his voice, and she turned to look at him thoughtfully, her wide blue eyes honest and direct. "Look, I know this isn't going to be easy. I never said it was. I can't deny that there's a special kind of chemistry between the two of us." As she said that, her voice softened and she had a moment of real doubt. But only for a moment. "That's what makes this so hard—and it's probably the very thing that's messing up my pictures. I'm up too close. I've got to get farther away. Please, please understand that nothing in my life has ever been more difficult." There was a catch in her voice and she lowered her lashes as she finished her plea. "Don't make this any harder for me than it already is."

Stoney was silent for a few minutes but his eyes never left her face. "Kiki Andrews, I think I'm in love with you. I've never felt this way before in my life. And I like it. I really do. And I want to understand you. I want that more than anything else in the world. But I think what you are asking of yourself is impossible." His voice dropped and he looked away for a moment, as if he hoped he wouldn't have to say what he knew he was going to say. "I'll do my best not to make it harder for you. But that's the most I can promise."

Kiki had some notion of how difficult that was for him to say, and inwardly, she was a bundle of conflicting emotions. Never had she been so confounded by her feelings, but she knew what she had to do, and she hoped her voice sounded more confident than she felt. "Okay, cowboy. You've got a deal." Smiling brightly, she stuck out her hand for a handshake.

Stoney hesitated for just a moment before clasping

her small hand in his larger one. "You drive a hard bargain," he said with a grin on his face. "Does this mean I can't walk you back to your hotel?"

Kiki had to laugh and the tension was broken for a moment. "I think that can be arranged. But you'll have to hurry. I don't have all day. I've got work to do."

Stoney was relieved that Kiki was beginning to sound like her old self again, and while he finished dressing, she gathered up her camera and equipment. In a very few minutes, they were both ready to walk out the door.

"Whoops," Stoney said, remembering something in the nick of time. "I've got to call Tully and tell him we're going to have company. If I know anything about Tully, he'll want to make sure he's got all the comforts of home on board The Bus. We've never had such a beautiful guest before," he added with a grin.

"Stoney, you promised," Kiki warned, her blue eyes flashing.

Immediately, Stoney assumed an expression of mock solemnity, and before she could finish her sentence, he said, "Just stating the facts, ma'am, just the facts. Besides, just think of all the wonderful pictures you can take on The Bus." His irrepressible good humor had obviously returned, and Kiki couldn't help smiling. This was not going to be easy, she thought ruefully as he made the necessary arrangements with Tully.

When he was sure everything would be taken care of, Stoney hung up the phone and turned to Kiki.

"Well, what are you waiting for? Let's get this show on the road." With that last remark, he opened the door and, very formally offering her his arm, led her down the hall to the elevators.

"Something tells me this is *not* going to work," Kiki said, trying to repress a smile as she looked over at Stoney's very serious expression. She had a moment of feeling really trapped, wondering if she had made the right decision after all. But she knew she really had no choice.

"What do you mean? Of course it'll work. It has to," Stoney said, and suddenly his expression was genuine. "It just has to."

Kiki looked at Stoney and smiled, an idea just starting to take form. "You're right," she said. "It has to work. But what I think we need is a little distance." She knew that unless she could somehow ease the tension and get things back on a lighthearted footing, it was never going to work. When the elevator door opened, she impulsively darted in ahead of Stoney. Fortunately the elevator was empty and, seeing the surprised look on Stoney's face, she laughed good-naturedly. "Last one down buys lunch," she said just as the door was closing.

"No fair!" Stoney called out, but Kiki had seen him quickly push the button for the other elevator, and she knew the race was on.

When Stoney's elevator finally stopped on the first floor and the door opened, Kiki was waiting for him in the elegant lobby, a mischievous look on her face and her camera poised for the shot. Before Stoney had a chance to say a word, she quickly snapped the shutter three times in rapid succession.

"Time for me to get back to work," she said blithely, laughing at his surprised expression.

"Fine, fine," Stoney teased, "just remember, all work and no play—" He quickly ducked the punch she aimed in his direction. Laughing, they set off arm in arm, ready for the new day.

6

～～～～～～～～～

Kiki stretched sleepily, lulled by the gentle motion of The Bus. She could sense light coming in behind her closed eyes, but she was reluctant to wake up. She stirred a bit, reached out for Stoney's form beside her on the long comfortable seat, and when her hand touched empty air, she woke up quickly. Where had he gone? For that matter, where had everybody gone? A brief survey of The Bus showed that it was virtually empty, though surely someone had to be driving it. Making her way to the front of the bus, she found Stoney whistling merrily, turning into a long dirt road off the highway.

"Good morning," she said sleepily. "Where are we?"

"Almost home, love, almost home," he replied, giving her a lazy smile. "Wait'll you see my place. You're bound to get some good pictures there."

"Your place?" Kiki asked. "Where are the rest of the guys?"

"Well, honey, I'm afraid you slept through most of the night. We've dropped them all off for a few days of R & R before the trip to Nashville. I figured you'd better come along with me to the end of the line."

Kiki laughed, happy to be alone with him, curious about seeing his house, though a trifle uneasy at the prospect of spending a few days alone with him. How would they ever keep from breaking their pledge not to be lovers?

They drove down the winding dirt road in companionable silence, caught up in the spell of the early morning and the beauty of the landscape before them. Kiki had been away from home so long that she had forgotten how beautiful the Texas Hill Country really was. Now, as she surveyed the modest spread that Stoney called home, it all came back to her in a rush. The gently rolling hills were green and lush, and she thought she spied the sparkling blue of a rushing stream or river down the hill. It seemed so quiet—all they could hear in the early morning light were the sounds of birds and insects, buzzing in harmonious concert.

Rounding a bend in the road, Stoney pulled The Bus up in front of a stone cottage, obviously built out of rock indigenous to the area. It was small yet picturesque, hardly what Kiki would have expected as the country retreat of a famous singing star. The long, narrow wooden porch was lined with potted plants, and a comfortable porch swing swayed gently in the cool breeze. Kiki thought she had never seen such an inviting house.

"Like it?" Stoney asked, turning off the engine and, setting the brake, looking down at her with a quizzical smile.

"Oh, it's lovely," Kiki breathed, returning a wide grin. "I just can't wait to see the inside."

"No sooner said than done," Stoney replied, opening the door and giving her a hand down off the high seat. "I just hope you like the inside as well."

Nothing Kiki had seen from the outside would have prepared her for the spacious interior which met her gaze upon entering the lovely house. The entire inside was done in crisp, clean white with stone floors downstairs and plush white carpet upstairs. Nothing detracted from the clear view of the river, afforded by the back wall of the house, which was a long series of glass windows and sliding doors. The house was built into the side of the hill, so the back wall looked down to the gently rolling river at the bottom. The furniture was new but comfortable —huge leather chairs and sofas and a fireplace dominated the living room. Kiki could see a kitchen and dining room off to one side.

"I've never seen anything like it!" She turned to Stoney with a new appreciation of his taste. "This is simply spectacular."

"Glad you like it," Stoney said nonchalantly, though it was clear that he was pleased she liked it. "It's my dream house. It took a lot of time and money to pull it together, but it's worth it. And it takes some effort to keep it going—I have a housekeeper come in every few days and my brother takes care of the grounds and animals. I like to spend as much time here as I can, though. It's the one place where I feel most myself. Think you can get some good shots here?"

"Oh, yes," Kiki laughed. "It will be a pleasure."

"Well, that's fine," Stoney said, his hand covering a yawn. "But it will just have to wait until later. I haven't slept all night, so I'm going to hit the hay for a while. You're welcome to join me—" The suggestion was tempting but Kiki lifted an eyebrow, warning him not to push.

"No thanks." Kiki tried to make her refusal gentle. "I'll just look around, if that's all right." She didn't see how she could hold out much longer under the circumstances, but it felt so good to be in his home that she forgave him for managing to get her alone.

"Sure, make yourself at home," Stoney said sleepily. "You should find everything you need, I'm sure. My housekeeper said she'd stock the kitchen, so just look around. And there are records and books if you get tired of exploring outside."

"Thanks." Kiki smiled as she stood on tiptoe to peck him on the cheek. "Now you get some rest, cowboy."

"Well, good night then, little lady," Stoney drawled as he went down the hall. "And remember, if you decide to join me, the invitation's still open."

"I'll keep that in mind," Kiki breathed softly as he turned into the doorway. "I'll certainly keep that in mind." With that thought, she went into the kitchen in search of something to munch on, having realized that it was midmorning and she hadn't had a thing to eat since the night before. She looked into the meticulously kept cabinets and found coffee, put a pot on to simmer, and rummaged around until she found some fresh *pan dulce,* a Mexican pastry. In the refrigerator, she found cantaloupe, already sliced, and she settled down at the long table to enjoy her simple breakfast, relishing the lovely view of the river. She could see Waco running along its edge— like his master, he seemed happy to be home.

Tidying up after herself, Kiki decided to look at the house first. The living room was made for living— with the large comfortable furniture grouped around the fireplace. A wall of shelves opposite the windows was filled with books, ranging from the latest in contemporary fiction to a set of biographies of famous composers to many large technical books on engineering. One whole section of the shelf was taken up with an elaborate stereo system and a vast record collection, again showing an incredible range of taste—everything from Bach to Hank Williams. Kiki shook her head. This man was certainly a challenge. No wonder she was having such a hard time photographing him. Just when she thought she'd figured him out, she saw another facet of his personality. Maybe that was also the source of his attraction for her. He was complicated and interesting. He was a challenge—that was it. Stoney Blue was probably the biggest challenge she had ever faced in her life. And she was beginning to be really pleased with her photographs of him. Maybe the distance they had maintained had helped, but simply realizing that something was wrong had also helped her correct it. Since she was already on the road with

Stoney, Sid had said she might as well cover the trip to Nashville. Photographing Stoney here in his beloved Hill Country home would be a bonus, she was sure.

She moved softly down the hall, not wanting to disturb his sleep, but curious to see the rest of the house. The hall led to four rooms—three bedrooms and a room that Stoney obviously used as a studio, for it was lined with musical instruments, including a grand piano. One wall was filled with sophisticated tape recording equipment, and the whole room, like all those of the back side of the house, looked down over the hill toward the river. From the studio, Kiki could see a barn off down the other side of the hill, and there were two horses grazing peacefully.

She looked in on Stoney as she went back down the hall. He was stretched out in a white bedroom, his clothes flung about the room. The covers were tumbled about his shoulders, and Kiki couldn't keep a fond smile from softening her features as she looked down at him. No one had the right to be that attractive—even when he was asleep. She fought back the urge to tenderly kiss his cheek, and left the room. The temptation to join him in the big soft bed was almost too hard to resist, especially when she thought about him lying there naked underneath the covers. She knew that body—knew its delights and pleasures all too well—and cut off here from the rest of the world as they were, she could feel the physical pull that existed between them.

And why shouldn't we be attracted to each other? she thought to herself. We're normal, healthy adults with a keen interest in living. There would be something the matter with us if we weren't attracted to each other under these circumstances.

Quietly letting herself out the back door, Kiki strolled along the deck to the stairs that led to the grass below. Waco came racing up the hill from the riverbank, glad to see her and ready to play. Kiki found a ball and the two of them had a spirited game of fetch, leaving her feeling refreshed and alert and glad of the exercise. Finally, she struck out toward the barn, Waco at her side, and went over to look at the horses, two lovely chestnut bays who came over to the fence and nuzzled her hand gently in search of sugar or some special treat.

The strain of the long trip was beginning to catch up with her, though, and she decided to go back to the house. Patting Waco on the head, she left him to play along the riverbank, and went into the living room, having decided to relax with a good book. But all too quickly she was overcome with fatigue, and she stretched out along the leather sofa for a nap.

She was awakened by a gentle nuzzling at her cheek. "Mmmm," she sighed sleepily, knowing only that whatever it was, it felt good. She felt soft lips trace a line along her cheek, and then she became aware of a rough beard teasing the sensitive skin of her neck. She didn't want to wake up; she only wanted this delicious feeling to continue. "Mmmmm," she said again.

"That should be my line," came Stoney's gravelly voice, jarring her into consciousness. "Mmmmm, you look good enough to eat."

Kiki opened her eyes to see his familiar, dear face

looking tenderly down at her. He had obviously showered and changed, for she could smell the scent of soap and male cologne, and the sensation was so overpoweringly pleasant that she allowed herself to nestle even more securely into the comfort of his arms. He had stretched his long frame out next to her on the large sofa and his hand trailed along the waistband of her designer jeans, gently teasing the soft skin of her flat stomach before traveling upward underneath her shirt to cup a soft breast in the palm of his hand. Kiki murmured her delight, knowing that it was pointless to resist him—especially since she was trapped between his warm body and the back of the sofa. And she was certainly not uncomfortable, she had to admit.

Kiki reveled in the sensations of her arousal as Stoney's lips captured hers. His tongue sought the soft interior of her mouth and she found herself relishing the tantalizing movement of his tongue, all the more so when she explored his mouth with her own. The kiss seemed to last forever, but it didn't keep Kiki from becoming aware that Stoney was gently massaging her breasts all the while. Her nipples hardened to rosy buttons as he teased them between thumb and forefinger, first one, then the other, until she was almost unbearably aroused.

When his fingers slipped to the zipper of her jeans, she had a momentary impulse to stop him before this interlude reached its inevitable conclusion, but she simply couldn't. The last couple of days, days in which she had insisted on pretending that she and Stoney were not lovers, had simply been too difficult. It was a farce to deny the sizzling attraction that existed between them, and Kiki was too honest with herself to deny her own nature. She wanted Stoney —she had wanted him from the first moment she saw him. And now, now that they were alone, it was simply pointless not to surrender to what they both desired so passionately.

She began to explore his body with her hands and mouth, unbuttoning the front of his western shirt to toy with the rough curling chest hair that met her inquisitive touch. Stoney groaned at her boldness, delighted by the possessiveness of her gesture. "I can think of a better place for this," he murmured softly, his deep voice sending thrills of sensual delight next to her ear.

"Oh, can you?" she teased. "But are you really sure you want to make the effort to move?"

He laughed down at her. "Why you little tease!" Rising from the sofa with a groan, he extended a hand to pull her to her feet, and when she smiled up at him lazily, he swooped down and picked her up in his arms, carrying her down the hall to the bedroom.

When Stoney placed her on the bed, he gently bent over her, tugging at buttons and zippers, removing her clothing until she was completely exposed before his appreciative gaze. "I love to look at you," he said in a husky voice. "Has anyone ever told you just how beautiful you really are, Kiki?"

Exulting in the power she felt to arouse him, she couldn't resist the urge to tease him just a little bit more. "Why yes, I think they have," she drawled, feigning thoughtfulness. "But no one quite like you has ever mentioned it before."

Stoney laughed at her again, but this time there

was a threatening undercurrent to his apparent humor. "Then I can see I'll just have to be more memorable than anyone else in other ways as well." Quickly stripping off his shirt and jeans—and Kiki saw with a start that he was *only* wearing jeans—he lowered himself to the bed beside her and proceeded to claim her body for his own, renewing the passion that had always flickered between them, banking the embers with his kisses until they fanned into flame.

Any impulse Kiki might have had to tease him quickly vanished under his passionate ministrations and all the laughter died in her throat as Stoney drove her to further heights with every kiss, every touch of his sensitive fingers. She was soon writhing under the exquisite torment of his teasing caresses. His lips kissed every feature of her face, and his tongue invaded the sensitive recesses of her delicate ears, then traveled lower to trail along the exposed skin of her throat.

Far from being without recourse of her own, Kiki set about inflicting her own brand of delightful torture on her passionate tormentor, her fingers caressing his beard while her lips worked a magic of their own on the pulse beating in the column of his throat. Relaxing the intensity of his onslaught upon her senses for a moment, Stoney lay back, delighting in her exploration of his body. Gently raising his hand to her lips, she gently kissed his fingers, taking them into her mouth in a gesture which was every bit as provocative as she intended for it to be.

"Kiki, you're driving me crazy," he groaned, and his mouth descended to her breasts, claiming first one then the other until her rosy nipples were peaks of desire, aching with the need to be pressed against that strong masculine chest. As his mouth sought the delights of her feminine flesh, she surrendered completely to her need for him, without a thought of the future. To live now, in this moment, was enough.

And when Stoney suspended his male length above Kiki in the instant before he took complete possession of her, she could only look at him with affirmation in her eyes—an affirmation that was the true reflection of what she felt in her heart. There was no holding back for either of them.

Stoney gently rocked her to fulfillment, his tempo gradually increasing to match her own quick ascent. His was the melody, hers was the harmony, and together they made of their love for each other a symphony of sensual pleasures. He played her body as if it were a delicate instrument, and Kiki found herself responding to every nuance of the music between them. When it was over, and they both lay still entwined, their passion spent but still lingering in their awareness, Kiki thought that she had never known such joy. Stoney gently cuddled her in his arms, both of them drifting off to sleep, secure in the knowledge that they would awaken in each other's arms.

The long shadows of the afternoon were lengthening when Kiki woke up after her deep sleep. She opened her eyes to see Stoney propped on one elbow observing her with affection in his blue eyes. "Hello, love," he said softly.

"Hello yourself." Kiki smiled. "Been awake long?"

"Just long enough to get a good look at you while

you're asleep—and what a sight it was!" He laughed. "You looked so innocent. No one would ever believe me if I said how sexy you could be when awake!"

"Maybe I'd better go back to sleep then!" Kiki said tartly, though she was pleased at the compliment. "I'd be safer asleep, I think."

"Don't count on it," Stoney said menacingly. "I have ways of waking you up—a lot of ways that I'm sure you'd like."

"I know." Kiki smiled contentedly. "I seem to recall your waking me up a few hours ago on the sofa. If memory serves me, that's how I ended up right here."

"Right!" Stoney said. "Glad you remember. Now, where do we go from here? Or do we? We could just stay here for the duration, you know."

"No, thanks," Kiki said firmly, sitting up and pulling the sheet across her breasts in a show of modesty that she knew was totally unnecessary, but if the look in Stoney's eyes was any indication, she needed to act quickly or they would never get out of bed. Not that that would be so bad, she said to herself, but just then her stomach growled, and both of them laughed.

"I'm hungry too," Stoney admitted, getting out of bed and pulling on his jeans. "Why don't I check out the refrigerator and I'll meet you in the kitchen?"

"Okay," Kiki agreed, her eyes following him fondly as he walked out of the room, her gaze lingering on his broad shoulders. She hopped out of bed, wrapping the sheet around her and went into the living room to find her small suitcase. Fifteen minutes later, after a revitalizing shower, she joined him at the long table in the kitchen, where he had set out a small feast for the two of them.

"My, my," Kiki laughed admiringly. "You do think of everything." She looked over the assortment of fruits and cheeses and crackers with pleasure. "I want to eat everything in sight."

"Well, help yourself," Stoney said, pushing a plate in her direction. "Just save room for dessert." He laughed, pointing at his own chest. "You should always save the best for last."

Kiki had to laugh as she began to relax and enjoy the food. It was so different to be alone with Stoney like this, momentarily free from the pressure of the next show as well as the presence of the other members of the band. Granted, she had to admit that she had enjoyed being with him in Houston and Austin, but this was different. She somehow felt that now she was seeing the man as he truly was, not as the thousands of fans saw him. And she liked what she saw. She liked it very much—possibly even too much. If she hadn't already lost her heart to this man, she knew that it was just a matter of time.

"What now?" Stoney asked when it was obvious that they had both eaten all that they could hold. "How about a short ride? I don't know when the horses were exercised last, and it would probably do us both good to get some fresh air—not that I'm complaining about the indoor sports. What do you say?"

"Sounds great," Kiki agreed, deciding for the moment to let the reference to indoor sports pass without a smart comeback. "If I hadn't eaten so much and if it weren't so cold, I'd want to go for a swim in the river, so a horseback ride sounds perfect."

"Great!" Stoney said. "Let's get going. We can have a nice ride, then I'll fire up the barbecue pit and cook steaks for dinner."

"Got it all planned, don't you?" Kiki teased, though she found his enthusiasm contagious.

"Not quite," Stoney replied with sudden seriousness. "I couldn't have planned this, Kiki. This is just perfect."

"It is, isn't it?" Kiki agreed softly, knowing that they were both caught in the spell of being together in this intimate setting. "Well, let's get on with it, then, though I have to warn you I haven't been on a horse since I was a teenager—and I should also warn you that I'm going to insist on taking my camera along. I have a job to do, remember?"

"Right," Stoney said, "and besides, my horses are terribly photogenic."

Laughing and joking, they made their way to the barn, Waco tearing out of the woods to trail along at their heels. The sun was slowly sinking in the west, its fiery redness reflected on the gently flowing river. Kiki thought she'd never seen such a perfect setting. She couldn't help comparing Stoney as he was now with the Stoney she had seen on the road, and she couldn't help admiring the way he had so successfully integrated the two areas of his life. He was certainly a complex man, she reflected, even for one so young. Now don't go turning into Mother Hubbard, she admonished herself, it's not like you're exactly over-the-hill yourself. It had been days since she had given any thought to the difference in their ages, and she was glad to discover that it seemed very insignificant for the moment.

While Stoney saddled up the horses for their ride, Kiki took out her camera and began photographing him. She admired the way his hands moved with swift confidence on the horses, fastening bridles, bits and saddles with smooth grace. She was almost sorry when the horses were saddled up, for she had honestly enjoyed the photo session, but she put her camera away with good grace, content that she was back at work.

"You take Lady," Stoney said, handing her the reins and waiting patiently to see if she needed a hand up. "I'll take Lightning here and then we'll be off."

Kiki, praying that her experience riding as a teenager would come back to her, was pleased when she managed to climb into the saddle unassisted. "With a name like Lightning, you'd *better* take him," she said and laughed over at Stoney, who was mounting the beautiful animal. "I'm afraid I'm a little rusty."

"Doesn't matter," Stoney assured her. "We'll take it easy until you feel comfortable."

The two of them started at a brisk walk along the riverbank, chatting companionably above their horses' heads. "I'm glad you like this place," Stoney said. "It's my pride and joy. I always knew that I wanted to live in the Hill Country, and it took some time to find the right place. But when I first saw this little spread, I knew it was for me."

"It *is* lovely," Kiki admitted, reluctant to acknowledge how much being in the Hill Country was making her homesick for Texas. "Sometimes, when I'm back here, I can't believe I actually live in New York—the two places just seem worlds apart."

"Well, they are worlds apart," Stoney said reasonably, "but I can tell you one thing. I wish you didn't live in New York City—I wish you lived right here with me."

Kiki smiled at him, grateful for the compliment, yet unwilling to let him know just how much she wished she lived here with him too. Though she knew that would never be—the two of them simply lived in different worlds, that was all. But she also knew she could be content with stolen hours like these. Stoney was too wonderful to resist—she realized she wanted him on any terms, but she wasn't sure how they could work things out. Sighing, she decided simply to enjoy the time they had together. Every hour, every day seemed like a precious gift—a gift that she knew would be withdrawn all too soon.

As they approached the edge of an open field, Kiki urged Lady into a brisk trot, thinking that the exercise would at least take her mind off the time when she and Stoney would have to be parted. She simply wasn't up to any more heavy discussions about their relationship—she only knew that she wanted to savor every moment they had together.

"Hey," Stoney called after her. "I thought you said you were a little rusty!"

"I am," she teased over her shoulder, "but it's all coming back to me now!"

The two of them raced along the open field until their horses were winded and Kiki's cheeks were flushed with the cool air as well as the exercise. Finally, as if by silent consent, they turned their horses and headed back to the stable.

"I'll take care of the horses," Stoney offered. "You go on up to the house and freshen up a bit. Then if you'll make a salad, I'll see about starting the fire for the steaks. Hungry?"

"You know it!" Kiki assured him. "Remember, I'm the girl with the hearty appetite."

"So you are," Stoney laughed. "So you are."

Kiki had already made a huge green salad and wrapped two potatoes in foil for baking when Stoney came in for the steaks. "Looks like you've been doing some hot work," she said as she handed him a glass of sangria.

"I have," Stoney admitted, "but the horses are curried and the fire's ready. Why don't you bring your drink out on the deck and join me?"

Kiki followed him out to the deck, gratefully accepting the lawn chair he offered her, for she found that her leg muscles were protesting a bit after the vigorous ride. They sipped their sangria in companionable silence, making small talk about the beautiful sunset and the view of the river. Kiki knew that she had never known such quiet joy and contentment. After a delicious dinner, they cleaned up the dishes like old friends, and when Stoney led her to the small fire he'd laid in the living room and handed her a snifter of brandy, she made no protest, joining him on the fur rug in front of the fire in silent contentment.

"You're beautiful in the firelight," Stoney murmured, running his long fingers through her hair.

"You're beautiful on horseback, too, but then I think I told you you're the most beautiful woman I've ever seen, haven't I?"

"Maybe you have," Kiki said quietly, "but tell me again. I like to hear you say it." And she turned her head upward for his kiss.

As if by tacit agreement, they both placed their drinks on the small ledge in front of the fireplace and went easily, gracefully, into each other's arms. Both of them smelled of wood smoke and horses, good strong animal smells, but that didn't seem to matter —only their closeness mattered. Kiki found herself wishing that every day could end like this, in Stoney Blue's arms.

She looked up at his face in the firelight, noting with tenderness the way the light brought out the golden highlights of his hair and beard. She couldn't know that Stoney was admiring her in much the same way, thinking that she was a lovely golden girl who had wandered into his life and who couldn't be allowed to escape him. They were perfect together— they both seemed to know it instinctively. There was no need to talk about it.

Stoney gently kissed every feature of her upturned face, and Kiki lay back with pleasure, allowing him to caress her until she could stand it no longer. Her fingers sought the buttons of his western shirt, teasingly, slowly unbuttoning each one until his tanned skin was naked and golden in the firelight. He quickly followed suit, pulling off her t-shirt so that her breasts were bare against his strong chest. They lingered that way for a while, Stoney caressing her breasts with his lips and hands, murmuring husky endearments in the intervals between kisses. Kiki ran her fingers along his strong manly torso, teasing his male nipples until they, like her own, had hardened to peaks.

Wordlessly, each turned aside to remove the rest of the clothing which now seemed such an encumbrance. And when they were both finally naked, they came together in a passion which was all the more satisfying for its lack of self-consciousness. Lips, tongues, fingers—all worked their unique magic as Stoney and Kiki drove each other on to greater and greater heights of arousal and need. Kiki, her back pressed into the soft fur of the rug, looked up at Stoney's magnificent form towering above her, and knew that there was no holding back—that this man had somehow made his mark on her, that she was now his—and that was all there was to it. She accepted the knowledge gracefully, as if it had been inevitable from the very first moment they had met.

Stoney gently came to her, then as if he could hold back no longer, he gave way to every passionate impulse in his nature and surrendered to the violent need he had for her. His strokes increased in depth and urgency, and Kiki found herself matching her tempo to his rhythm, her need every bit as desperate as his. When the moment of fulfillment finally came, they were both gazing at each other with wide-open eyes, and the love and the joy mirrored there was proof of their delight. After a brief moment of silence, Stoney sighed his satisfaction and rolled over on his back. Kiki followed him in a single graceful movement, stretching her length along the top of his body.

Later, basking in the glow of fire, Kiki laughed at

her own reservations about being on this trip with Stoney. We have three more days at the ranch, she told herself, sleepy with contentment. Three more days just like this one. Do human beings really deserve such joy?

As if he had read her thoughts, Stoney spoke in his deep gravelly voice. "Three more days, my love. Only three more days. Let's make them last a lifetime."

Kiki could only nod with pleasure. She would think about it. She would definitely think about it.

7

Kiki carefully removed the lens cap from her camera and tiptoed in closer to take advantage of a perfect shot. The recording studio had given her lots of ideas for pictures and she was pleased with the work she had done that morning, but it was getting late and she realized that her stomach was growling. Bending down on one knee to get a panoramic shot of the men in the control room bent over the sound panel with expressions of intense concentration, she clicked the shutter, satisfied that it would be an interesting photo, even though the subjects weren't nearly as photogenic as Stoney Blue.

But then who is? she mused to herself. Tiptoeing softly to a better vantage point, she shot a few more pictures of Stoney and the band, though she knew that she already had more than enough for the photo-essay. In fact, the assignment was already at an end, though she hadn't told Stoney yet. That was only one of the things on her mind at the present moment.

She hadn't been surprised when Sid had called that morning, raving about her latest batch of photographs. "I don't know what you're doing that's right, but it's something special!" he had said admiringly. She had known they were good when she developed them—really good, not just okay. What she hadn't been prepared for was the news that Images, a fashionable photography gallery in SoHo, wanted to give her a one-woman show the very next month!

"They really want you, Kiki," Sid had reassured her. "And you know it's the chance of a lifetime. As much as I'd hate to see it happen, it could be a way for you to be recognized for the artist you are. You *know* you're more than just a photo-journalist. You're the best."

Kiki had responded with typical modesty, but she knew that Sid was sincere in his praise. As she had promised him, she called the gallery owner and set the day for the show. Now the only problem was breaking the news to Stoney. Granted, they had both known that she would have to leave sometime, but somehow neither of them had expected that sometime to be so immediate.

She looked over at Stoney and felt all of her resolve melt away. She didn't want to leave him— she really didn't. But if she were honest with herself, she'd have to admit that her life simply was taking her on to other places—and right now the most important place for her was New York. She would just have to tell him when she could and hope that he would understand.

Stoney looked over in her direction and smiled at her. She blew him a kiss, hoping that her cheerful pose was convincing. She had to marvel at the man's patience. They had been in the red brick studio on Music Row in Nashville since early that morning, and had been hard at work on cuts for their first LP. Through it all, Stoney had been meticulous about the smallest detail, but he hadn't once gotten short-tempered or irritable. She really wasn't surprised though, for she had always known that Stoney had star quality, from the first moment she'd met him. The man was a true professional. He'd have to understand that she was a professional as well.

It was just that there was so little time. Sid wanted her to leave tomorrow at the latest. She knew that she had hit her stride again, that the black and white shots of Stoney and the band were some of her best work. The few days she had spent with the band in Austin, and then alone with Stoney at his home in the Hill Country, had fueled her creative energies, and she knew that this was evident in her work. Thinking back on their time together at the ranch, a fond smile lighted her face. It had been idyllic.

The trip from Texas to Tennessee had been a pleasure too, though it had taken several days, for the band had scheduled appearances in Little Rock and Memphis. Kiki had taken some wonderful new photographs of people and places along the way— shots that weren't part of the photo-essay, but for her own sense of artistic satisfaction. She was anxious now to get back to her own darkroom in New York, to really devote some serious time to her work. She was torn between the desire to continue this open-ended journey with Stoney and the need she felt to return to her own life. There were moments when she was beginning to feel a little closed in. From time to time the old fear that she was just another groupie following the band reared its ugly head and she found herself becoming more and more restless.

In spite of the pleasure she derived from this relationship, she didn't see that there was any future in it. She and Stoney were both prisoners of their careers, and neither one of them really wanted it any other way. She knew she had to—needed to—get away, but she wasn't at all sure Stoney would understand. Even though he took a great deal of interest in her work, she worried that he might not be so interested if she were halfway across the country.

Well, she told herself, slipping off the stool and stretching, that's just something she would have to find out. After all, she already had plane reservations for tomorrow night after the show. She had to tell him sometime. There was no question in her mind that Stoney was a special person in her life, and her feelings for him were stronger than she had thought possible. But she had to be honest with herself—he wasn't the first man she'd been involved with, and while she knew he was somehow different from all the others, she still wasn't about to be tied down. She had a life of her own and it was time she got back to it. She'd been living Stoney's life too long.

Roused from her reverie by her stomach growling again, Kiki glanced down at her watch and was surprised to discover that it was well after two. And no one had had a thing to eat since breakfast! As if he could read her thoughts, Stoney signaled to the band to take a break, calling a halt to the men in the control room. Before she knew it, he was at her side.

"Hello there, cowboy," she said softly, a smile on her face. There was something about this man that never failed to arouse her.

"Are you already through shooting for today?" Stoney asked, the expression on his face one of genuine interest.

"Yeah. Just finished. Everything's great. Are you getting tired? Seems like an awfully long session to me." She asked as much out of politeness as anything else, for it would be obvious even to a complete stranger that Stoney was loving every minute of it.

"Oh, no, no, I'm fine. But I worry about you having to sit here and wait for us. It can't be much fun for you, especially if you're through taking pictures." Stoney looked down at her blue eyes as if to make sure she was really all right.

"I'm okay. I've never seen a recording session before and it's fascinating. It's not what I'd want to do day in and day out, but for one day, it's great. But are you sure I can't do something for you? Are you hungry? Thirsty? I have to admit that a walk in the sunshine right about now sounds pretty good to me. I could get everyone some lunch." She hoped she didn't sound too eager to get away. She was feeling a little cooped up though she didn't want Stoney to know that. She didn't want to add to the pressure he was already facing, though she knew she would have to eventually.

"Oh, that sounds great! Are you sure you don't mind? I know we're all starving. But isn't it too much trouble?" Stoney's face looked a little relieved at her suggestion.

"Not a bit. C'mon, let's go take orders." With this, she turned and headed over to the rest of the band. A few minutes later, Stoney was walking her to the door. "Now, let's see if I've got this straight—two hamburgers with cheese, one with onions, two corn dogs and a large Frito pie. Are you sure Ramsey's really serious about that?" She laughed as she looked up at Stoney's smiling face.

"Don't worry about Ramsey—he's got a stomach made of iron. He can eat anything—and has. You're sure you won't have any trouble now?" He stood with both hands on her shoulders, his face filled with concern.

"Don't be silly, Stoney. I've been all over the world on my own. I'm sure I can find a hamburger place that's right around the corner. We passed it this morning driving over, remember? It isn't even two blocks away. But I may take a little extra time— there's a store or two I'd like to browse in—that is, if you guys could hold out a few extra minutes. I think the fresh air will do me good." She stood on tiptoe to peck him on the cheek. "It's okay, it really is. I'm a big girl, remember?"

"Well, I won't argue with that," Stoney said with a laugh. "Just don't be gone *too* long. I like having you around."

"You bet. Now go on back and get to work. I'll see you later." With a cheerful wave and a bright smile, she turned and walked down the street.

Sure enough, the bright afternoon sunshine was just what Kiki needed after being in the studio. She strolled down Music Row, with its cluster of red brick buildings, humming a happy tune under her breath. Turning onto the thoroughfare, she browsed through a few souvenir stands, bought a few presents for Sid and her friends in New York and finally made her way to the hamburger stand which was exactly where she remembered.

Sitting on a bench outside while she waited for the order, Kiki felt a brief surge of happiness, followed by an inevitable current of regret. Up until now, everything had seemed so perfect, and she knew she would always look back on this time with Stoney as a romantic idyll in her life, something she had neither expected nor dreamed of. It was such a shame that it was all going to end so quickly, so abruptly. She dreaded breaking the news to Stoney, anticipating his response. He would never understand, she knew that.

But he *should!* He was a professional, an artist with plans and demands of his own! He needed to recognize that her professional interests extended far beyond a photo-essay on Stoney Blue for *Lifestyle* magazine. Even Sid seemed to understand that, and he encouraged her to try her wings—even at the risk of losing her entirely. But then, she reflected, she wasn't in love with Sid. Far from it. And she knew she was hopelessly in love with Stoney Blue. Time to get out, she told herself firmly, time to cut your losses and move on.

"Oh, miss! Miss!" the kid in the window of the

hamburger stand must have been trying to get her attention for a few minutes. "Your order's ready."

"Sure, sure!" Kiki snapped to with a jolt. "Thanks a lot!"

Walking back to the recording studio in the sunshine, Kiki felt her customary high spirits returning. No matter what happened, it would be all right. If things were meant to work out with her and Stoney, they would. If they weren't, then they simply wouldn't. She had her work, after all. That was all that mattered.

The atmosphere in the studio was festive when she returned—apparently things had been going well during her absence. "Food! Food!" they all chanted in unison when she arrived, and Kiki found herself responding to their good humor in kind. She doled out hamburgers and corn dogs and Ramsey's Frito pie, and sat down to join in the laughter that inevitably accompanied lunch with Stoney and the band. Even the technicians who'd been in charge of the recording session seemed to be in a good mood. "I think we've got a hit album on our hands," one of them said confidently. "Just a little more work, a week or so at the most, and we'll have this one in the bag."

A week! Kiki thought to herself, I couldn't possibly spend an entire week like this. I guess this is a good time to leave after all. At least Stoney will have other things on his mind, and maybe he won't miss me as much. She didn't want to admit to herself how much she would miss him.

After lunch, they decided to stop for the day, and

Stoney turned to Kiki with an inquisitive look in his eye. "How about a little sightseeing?" he asked. "We haven't had a chance to see much since we've arrived, and this afternoon seems as good a time as any. Besides, it would give me a chance to unwind before rehearsals tomorrow and the show tomorrow night. How does that sound to you?"

"Sounds great," Kiki readily agreed, glad for another chance to get out and see something of Nashville. She also welcomed the opportunity to spend some time alone with Stoney, though she dreaded the idea of telling him she was leaving. But it looked like today would be as good a time as any. Tomorrow he would be so wound up at the prospect of the show that it wouldn't be fair to tell him then.

Kiki and Stoney sent the band on in The Bus after they'd been dropped off in the heart of the city. "Here is where it all started," Stoney said to her as they emerged from The Bus in front of Ryman Auditorium. "For years, this had been the site of the Grand Ole Opry before they built Opryland. Think of all the great country-western stars who got their start right here. It's a shame it's not used more often, you know?"

"Well, it will certainly be in use tomorrow night," Kiki teased gently. "Stoney Blue and his band will fill the old place with music. That should make all the ghosts of the building feel as if they've returned to their former glory." She smiled up at him, relishing his pleasure in the very idea of playing in Ryman Auditorium. She had known it meant a lot to him, but now she was beginning to understand why.

They walked down the street and turned on

Broadway, heading down the street lined with tiny stores and restaurants and pawn shops with windows filled with musical instruments. She could see Tootsie's Orchid Lounge in the distance.

"That's what I love about Nashville," Stoney continued. "Everything just reeks of the history of country music. Like this, for instance," he said, steering her into a store. "This is Ernest Tubb's Record Shop. Just look at it!" he continued with boyish enthusiasm, leading her through rows and rows of records. "For years and years, this place has had a midnight Jamboree. A lot of the greats have been picking and grinning here at midnight. . . ." He reeled off a breathtaking list of the famous stars who had appeared there.

Kiki was fascinated with Stoney's knowledge of the city and she tried to be a good listener, but she was preoccupied with telling Stoney her news, finding just the right moment and place to tell him. They walked for what seemed like hours, exploring various parts of the city. It wasn't until they were strolling through beautiful Centennial Park that Kiki thought the time had come. They had stopped to rest near a giant concrete shell when she mustered her courage and began to speak.

"Listen, Stoney," she began hesitantly, then rushed on, determined to get it over with. "I had a long talk with Sid this morning, and the photo-essay on you and the band is almost complete and set to run in a few weeks." Seeing the expression on his face change, she hurried on before he could interrupt her. "And there's more—one of the most prestigious photographic galleries in New York called the magazine looking for me, and they've offered me a one-woman show next month. It's a last-minute thing, filling in for someone who couldn't get it together, but it's the chance of a lifetime and I just can't afford to pass it up. I've got to go home and get back to work."

The last words came out in a rush of anticipation— she knew that Stoney was going to object. And she was terribly vulnerable to any temptation to stay. Looking at the strong, sensitive face that had come to mean so much to her over the past few weeks, she realized that she was hurting him terribly, but she didn't know what she could do about it.

"Well, Kiki," he drawled slowly, obviously trying to give himself time to think before he spoke, "I can see that this is a once-in-a-lifetime chance for you, I can understand that, I really can. But I thought we were beginning to have some understanding between us. I thought we both knew that this was special, this thing between us, and I thought we were both starting to think of ways to make it permanent. I know that I can't talk you into staying here, though I wish I could, but I'm real sorry that you seem to think you have to go rushing off just when things were so right between us."

Even though Kiki responded to the feeling in his voice, she was angered by the assumption that she was *rushing off.* "Well, let me tell you, cowboy," she began, a little heatedly. "Before I met you, I had a pretty fine life. I had my work, and I had a good reputation for what I do. I have a loft in New York as well as a job at a magazine that I like a lot. And while it's been fun chasing you all over the South, I have to tell you that it's time I got back to my own life—my real life."

"I know all those things," Stoney said softly. "I really do. And I don't mean to belittle your life or your work before we met. I had somehow just hoped that you were thinking along different lines these days."

"Why do *I* have to be the one to think along different lines?" Kiki demanded, her anger really getting the better of her now. "Why can't *you?* I've taken a lot of time to be with you. Granted, some of it, a good deal of it, has been work on the photo-essay, but we both know that there was more to it than that. Why can't you take some time off and come back to New York with me for a while?" She knew when she asked the question that it was hopeless.

"Kiki, you know I can't do that right now," came the slow answer. "You heard that guy in the studio today. Another week and we'll have the album wrapped up. And you know I have the show to do tomorrow night."

"But what about after that?" Kiki asked softly, dreading the answer she knew would come.

"Honey, you know I can't do that," he answered with sadness in his voice. "We've got club dates lined up for the next few weeks solid. A tour can't be changed this late in the game. We were lucky to get a few days at the ranch. We were lucky to land in Nashville for this long—it's rare that a tour allows for so much time in a single place. It looks like our luck has run out, I'm afraid."

"You don't live your life by luck," Kiki retorted

scornfully. "You *make* luck. I just think that your career is more important to you right now than I am. Or else you'd be willing to change."

"I don't understand how you can expect me to cancel everything in the middle of a tour that's been booked for a long time," Stoney shot back, his sadness turning into anger. "And who's to say that my career is more important to me than yours is to you? After all, you're the one who's leaving."

Kiki knew that she was being unreasonable, as she had been the last time they had had this conversation, but there seemed to be no easy answers for the problems that were confronting them. And she knew, deep within herself, that she was being slightly selfish, for she wanted Stoney to *say* that her work was important too, even though she knew he felt that way.

"All right," Kiki said, her inherent sense of honesty coming into play. "You're right. I'm the one who's leaving. I'll admit that. But I still don't see why you couldn't come to New York for a visit at least. When the tour's over, maybe." She had to ask for one concession on his part.

"Maybe," Stoney allowed. "But I can't make any promises. When the tour's over, I've got to get back to Texas. I have responsibilities too, you know. And I have to tell you, Kiki, I don't like New York. I've been there a few times and I just don't like it. It makes me feel all closed in and crazy. I'm sorry but that's the way it is."

"Okay," Kiki said miserably. "We'll just have to wait and see." Inwardly she was still angry and depressed. Granted, she could understand how Stoney felt about New York, but she wasn't about to admit it. She wanted him to admit that somehow there might be the possibility of a relationship beyond this time and this place.

"It's not the end of the world, honey," Stoney said softly, putting his arm around her shoulders.

But Kiki was not to be won over so easily. "You're right, it's not," she said, and her voice took on a brittle quality. She refused to let him see how much this whole conversation bothered her. She had too much pride to let this man see how much he'd gotten to her. Besides—and this was always her last refuge when she was upset with Stoney—he was simply too young for her. After all, this success was new to him—and apparently, he hadn't had many serious relationships with women before. If he were just a little older and more experienced, perhaps he would have been less idealistic and more understanding. But no, he was young and he was hot and he was on the way up. There was no stopping him and, Kiki reflected, there was no slowing him down.

The two of them left the park and walked back toward downtown in a strained silence. When they reached the hotel where the band was staying, Stoney finally spoke. "Well, when are you leaving?" he asked, and his voice seemed resigned to the inevitable.

"Tomorrow night," Kiki said in clipped tones. "Right after the show. I've got the last flight out."

"Good," he said softly. "It will mean a lot to me to have you at the show."

"Happy to oblige," Kiki said coldly. "I aim to please." She disliked herself for the anger in her voice, but she couldn't help herself. She felt like she'd been gambling for high stakes and she'd just lost everything. Maybe Stoney was right—maybe their luck had run out.

8

·∞∞∞∞∞∞∞∞∞∞·

Hey, Kiki. Come on, give me a break," Stoney said with uncharacteristic irritation. "Let me practice, okay?" With that remark, he sighed and once again turned his attention to the guitar in his hands. He was not yet satisfied with a new arrangement, and Kiki knew he wanted to try it out on the Nashville audience.

"Sure thing, cowboy," Kiki said with what she hoped was a lighthearted response. Inwardly she was stunned by his curt tone of voice. Leaning over the back of the piano, she had just gotten a good close-up of Stoney deep in concentration. Sid might have had all the photographs he needed, but she couldn't resist a few more shots of Stoney and the band while they rehearsed for the show that night.

His temper had caught her off guard, and, with a

quick glance in Tully's direction, she slipped quietly off the stage as unobtrusively as possible. Tully returned her glance with a wink and a sympathetic shrug; she wasn't the only one surprised by Stoney's attitude.

Making her way to the back of the auditorium, Kiki found her leather camera bag where she had left it earlier. Putting away her camera and carefully securing the other equipment, Kiki made herself comfortable in the last row of wooden pews. She couldn't help feeling just a little hurt even though she knew Stoney was under a great deal of pressure. She had never seen a performance affect him in this way. But then Nashville was like no place else in the country for a musician. This was the big time. This was where it counted.

On top of all that, both she and Stoney had been on edge with each other since the day before when she told him Sid wanted her back in New York City. The photo-essay was finished, and there was nothing else for her to do. She had hoped Stoney would be as excited as she had been about the gallery in SoHo inviting her to have a show. But he hadn't understood how important it was to her. All he wanted was for her to stay on the road with him. She was almost sorry that she had agreed to stay another day and had made reservations for a late flight that night after the show.

Looking around the theater, Kiki understood why Tully had chosen this auditorium—it was the perfect setting for Stoney and the band. It wasn't too slick or gaudy, just down-home comfortable. Besides, it exuded country atmosphere. Originally built by a riverboat captain as a place for revivals, Ryman Auditorium still had some of its churchlike atmosphere, with rows of wooden pews and paper fans. There was a certain raw energy about the place— one couldn't help remembering that the Grand Ole Opry used to be broadcast live from this very spot. It seemed a much more appropriate place for Stoney than the circus-like atmosphere of Opryland across town.

Pushing an unruly curl of hair from her face, Kiki sighed. It wasn't surprising that she and Stoney were getting on each other's nerves. They had been together night and day since they left Houston, and such constant companionship was a new experience for her. And once she began to be satisfied with her photographs of Stoney—it hadn't taken her long to find her old knack—she was ready to move on. But being with Stoney was seductively easy, and one more day had turned out to be weeks.

She was afraid she might never get back to her own work if she stayed much longer—not that she had completely neglected it. She had actually found a new dimension to her skills. In desperation, she had started taking pictures of the countryside while they were still in Texas, and it had been exciting for her to discover that she had an artistic sense of something other than famous people. She loved the Texas Hill Country where Stoney had a house, and she felt a oneness with the wide-open landscape so familiar to her childhood. She planned to show these new Texas photographs in her show next month, and she hoped they would be as well-received as she expected them to be.

"You still speaking to me?" Stoney's soft drawl interrupted her reverie, and she was surprised to see him towering above her. She must have been miles away in her daydreaming.

"Sure thing." She grinned impishly up at him and motioned to the spot beside her. "Sit a spell."

"Thanks, Kiki. I wouldn't blame you if you didn't speak to me. I just don't know what's gotten into me today. I've jumped down everyone's throat. If I have any friends left after this show tonight, it'll be a miracle." He leaned over and kissed her gently on the lips. "I'm sure glad you're here. It means a lot to me."

"It's okay, Stoney. Don't give it another thought. This is an important show tonight. No one expects you to be Little Mary Sunshine all the time." This was Kiki's first real chance to visit alone with Stoney today. He had been up early and would have started rehearsing before breakfast except that Tully and the other guys had put up such a ruckus. Even now, in spite of his sincerely apologetic words, she could tell that he was still preoccupied. She knew this was no time for her to harbor hurt feelings.

"Yeah, I guess not," he said absentmindedly. He was already off in another world once again and was plainly not hearing a word she said. Suddenly his face brightened for a moment and a smile broke out across his face. "I got it!" he said, snapping his fingers excitedly.

Before Kiki had a chance to say "got what?"

Stoney had dashed back up on the stage, obviously wanting to try something out on his guitar.

The rest of the band had been taking a short break, but when they saw Stoney on the stage, they joined him, though not without some groans of mock displeasure and a little clowning around. In spite of all their shenanigans, Kiki could tell that they were eager to find out what he had up his sleeve.

Kiki was struck once again with the camaraderie that existed between the men, and all of a sudden she felt a twinge of envy—they were having fun doing what they wanted to do. She was on the outside looking in—and always would be. It came to her in a flash that Stoney was exactly where he should be just as she should be in New York City. Suddenly a little claustrophobic, Kiki gathered up her camera and equipment and slipped out of the auditorium. She didn't like what was happening to her and she was determined to nip it in the bud. She had never been envious of someone else's work, and she knew she wouldn't have been today if she had been as fully engrossed in her work as Stoney was in his. She had great respect for his talent and ambitions and she wanted a lot for him. But that did not mean sacrificing her own career.

Once out on the street in the bright sunshine, Kiki realized what a tangled set of complications their professional commitments made, and she saw that they were hopelessly imprisoned by their careers—and she knew she wouldn't have it any other way. Quickly, she walked the short distance back to the hotel. She wanted to finish packing her things before

Stoney came up to dress for the show. Even though she knew she had to leave, she was filled with a deep sadness—she loved Stoney and she knew he loved her. If only it had been some other place, some other time. Perhaps it would have been different—but she couldn't and wouldn't want to wish away their careers. Still, it was a bitter disappointment.

Waco greeted her enthusiastically when she opened the door to their adjoining hotel rooms. "Hello there, Waco," she said, stopping a moment to play with the shaggy-haired dog. "At least you're glad to see me. You know, Waco, it surely must be great to be a dog. Relationships don't ever get too complicated for you, do they? But then you don't want to be a fancy-dancy photographer when you grow up. Or a famous singer. You've got more sense than all of us put together. Yeah, atta boy. Go get this." The morning newspaper was still rolled up so Kiki tossed it across the room, much to Waco's delight. The dog raced across the room and eagerly brought the paper back to Kiki. She laughed and threw it again. Waco brought the paper back to Kiki once more, his tail wagging joyously.

Kiki sat down on the couch and pulled off her boots. Waco happily licked her toes and, after a few moments of play, settled down quite comfortably on the floor at her feet.

"Looks like we're in the same boat today. Here I am all by myself with no one but a great big friendly dog to talk to." She wiggled her toes and looked thoughtfully around the room. Surveying her sur-roundings, she noted the haste with which she and

Stoney had dressed this morning. The disarray made her wish for her own apartment in New York City. That wistful nostalgia surprised Kiki; she was quite accustomed to living out of a suitcase. But she'd been gone for a good while now, and she was ready to get back.

Getting up and hurrying across the large sitting room to her bedroom, she began to gather up her belongings. Since the assignment had stretched as long as it had, it was fortunate that Kiki had been such a thorough packer. Her color-coordinated wardrobe was highly versatile and there were several different ways to wear almost everything.

As she packed, she studied her wardrobe, trying to decide what to wear that night to the performance. Whatever she chose, it would have to be suitable for the late-night flight to New York. Finally, after much deliberation, she decided on a comfortable pair of khaki pants with a scoop-necked red silk blouse. If she wore her pearl necklace, the silk blouse would dress up the tailored pants and she could carry her navy blazer to wear on the plane. Satisfied with that choice, she quickly finished her packing. After what was beginning to feel like a long day, she was looking forward to a relaxing soak in a hot tub.

Checking the closets to make sure she hadn't left anything behind, she opened her cosmetic case for the bath oils she always carried with her and hurried into the luxurious bathroom to start her bath water. Stoney was bound to be back soon, and she wanted a few more minutes alone. Packing brought her that much closer to leaving, and the closer she was to that, the more her spirits fell. As much as she wanted to get back, and as much as she wanted to begin work on the show, she couldn't help feeling a great sense of loss. She had more fun with Stoney than she'd ever had with anyone—and more solid companionship. There was nothing they hadn't talked about. She was more at ease with him than with anyone she'd ever known.

It's not just a physical attraction, she mused to herself as she placed fresh lingerie on the vanity and slipped into the soothing water. The sweetly scented water was warm, and as she sank down in the bath, she blew a handful of bubbles across the tub. She knew there was more to this relationship than sex, although that too was special. If only their lifestyles and careers weren't so badly mismatched.

She sighed, realizing that she was once again going around in the same old circle and getting nowhere fast. Resolving to get off that horse, she quickly finished bathing. When she stepped out of the tub, she was delighted to find that she had left the tension of the day behind.

"Hello," she called from the bathroom. "I can practically hear Waco's tail wagging from in here." Securely wrapping the large fluffy towel around her slender frame, she met Stoney at the door.

He gave out a long, low whistle and his penetrating blue eyes missed nothing as he looked her over, obviously appreciative of what he saw.

"Hello, gorgeous," he said as he took her in his arms. "This looks like pretty good timing, I'd say." He kissed her, gently at first, but as her arms went around his neck in a natural response, the kiss took on a kind of urgency that surprised her. When he finally relinquished his hold on her, he said huskily, "I missed you. Thought maybe you'd left for good."

"You know better than that," she said playfully, pulling on his ears. "My plane doesn't leave for hours yet. And you know I wouldn't miss the show tonight for anything."

"I know, I know," Stoney whispered in her ear as he held her close once again. "But it was a good preview of what's to come. What am I going to do without you?"

"The same thing you did before we met—be a rising young country-western singer—break hearts all over the country. Besides, there's always the telephone. It's not like I'm going to Timbuktu, you know. New York City is only a few hours away by plane. We'll see each other often. It's going to be all right, really it is." She hoped her voice sounded more confident than she felt. At the moment, her customary optimism was badly floundering.

"Hey, I've got a great idea." Stoney kissed her firmly on the lips, holding her face in both his hands.

"What's that?" She looked up at him, her blue eyes wide with expectation.

"First, let's get out of the bathroom," Stoney said with a grin and, scooping her up in his strong arms, he carried her into the bedroom.

"You make me feel like a princess," she said, laughing as he gently laid her on the soft bed.

"You are a princess," Stoney said earnestly, looking down thoughtfully, his eyes locking with hers in a sensual gaze. "The fairest and the most wise and the—"

"Whoa now." Kiki laughed, putting her fingers to his lips, hushing him. "Don't you think you're going to extremes? Is that your great idea?"

"No, of course not." Stoney grinned impishly. "But now that I've got your attention, I think I'll save that for later. I've just had another great idea."

"Oh, you have, have you? And whatever could that be?" Kiki asked with feigned innocence. "Let me see if I can guess." She pretended to be thinking very hard.

"Okay, but you've only got three guesses." Stoney leaned over and kissed her neck tenderly, his hands loosening the towel wrapped around her voluptuous body.

Kiki felt herself becoming aroused as his hands moved gently over her body and a sensual wave swept through her. "Animal, vegetable or mineral," she whispered as she ran her fingers through his tousled hair.

"Is that your first question or are you just warming up?" Stoney asked in between tiny kisses over her neck and shoulder.

"Warming up," Kiki said with a chuckle, and she held him close, his mouth on the sensitive flesh above her breasts.

"Now you're talking." Stoney sat up and removed the towel easily, and as he spoke, his eyes and hands roamed her beautiful body that was already writhing seductively under his masterful touch.

Kiki closed her eyes as she succumbed to the

passions of the moment. When his mouth found her nipples she felt herself instinctively arch into his embrace and she knew she was hopelessly lost in his arms. But she didn't care. For the moment, she forgot that she would be leaving this man in only a few short hours. For the moment, she banished all the complications of their relationship from her thoughts. All she wanted was to continue this sweet lovemaking that she had become accustomed to. Later she would deal with the consequences.

Gently, ever so gently, she unbuttoned his shirt, and when her hands touched his bare skin and her fingers caught in the mass of hair on his chest, she felt a shiver of intense pleasure rack his strong body.

"Oh, Kiki," he whispered as his eyes met hers. "My darling, my darling." With that endearment he brought his mouth to hers in a crushingly passionate kiss, his tongue insistently parting her willing lips that he might eagerly explore the sweet recesses of her mouth.

For her part, Kiki slipped his shirt off completely and, moving her hands tenderly up and down his back, she felt the muscles rippling beneath the smooth sensitive flesh and she reveled in the intense pleasure of his skin against hers.

He began once more to kiss her neck erotically, and when she boldly began to undo his jeans he stood up and slowly finished undressing, his eyes feasting upon her aroused body with unabashed pleasure. His movements were unhurried as they each enjoyed their sensual knowledge of each other, and when their gaze finally locked in shameless desire, he came down beside her on the bed, his hands parting her legs and caressing her inner thighs until her slender legs stiffened with passion.

Just when she thought she could no longer stand the exquisite torture of his touch, his fingers and his mouth and tongue sought with complete abandon the delights of her flesh. Kiki moaned, her undulating body responding completely to his embrace. The sensitive skin stimulated with an intense pleasure was almost more than she could bear, she felt her entire body tremble with desire, and she pulled his face up until his eyes met hers. Never had she been so completely and exquisitely aroused as she was at this moment, and, sensing her need, he took possession of her body, claiming the ecstasy of their union with perfect timing and a natural rhythm that took her over the edge of rapture first, then finally he followed suit with a shudder of intense relief. They lay still in each other's arms. Neither wanted to break the spell of the moment; they were both exhausted. Kiki felt the heavy weight of his body on hers, and moved her hands slowly and tenderly on his back.

"For a great idea, that's not half bad," Kiki whispered in his ear.

"You like that, do you?" Stoney rolled over on his side, leaned his head on his elbow and looked down at her.

"That's the understatement of the year," Kiki answered, her finger tracing lazy circles on his chest.

"You know, I may be able to sing tonight after all," Stoney said with a grin. "I'm no longer all tied up in knots."

"The band's going to be relieved to hear that,"

Kiki retorted as she fluffed up the pillow under her head. "You've been something of a bear today."

"I know, and I'm sorry," Stoney said with genuine regret. "You know, I'm like a drug addict—I've gotten dependent on you and already I'm suffering from withdrawal symptoms."

"That's not good, Stoney, you know it's not. You don't need me to keep going—or at least I certainly hope you don't. You might as well get used to the idea because it's closing in on us." Sometimes Kiki found herself reacting irritably when she felt that Stoney couldn't let her go. She loved him, but she didn't want to feel like she was holding him up.

"I had another great idea," Stoney said with an impish grin. He pushed a stray curl from her face.

"I was beginning to think you'd forgotten all about it," Kiki responded in what she hoped was a light-hearted tone of voice as she returned his grin. She was a little relieved to be off the subject of her departure.

"Nope. I was just saving the best for last." Stoney had a thoughtful look on his face.

"I don't see how that's possible," Kiki said with a knowing smile. "But let's have it."

"Well, I've been thinking," Stoney stammered nervously. "That is, what I wish—" His voice broke off again and he was having trouble looking her in the eye.

"Hey, I don't believe what I'm hearing. You sound like you've got stage fright." Kiki teased him playfully, hoping to ease the tension emanating from him.

"I'm making this harder than it is," Stoney said, shaking his head. Abruptly he continued; there was a

147

new force and determination in his voice when he went on. "I want you to marry me. Will you marry me, Kiki?"

Yes, screamed a silent voice inside her head. Tell him yes. And even though that was her initial reaction, Kiki remained silent. You know it's what you want, the voice went on, you know you love him and he loves you. Make it easy on yourself for once. Give in, let it happen, say yes. Kiki was sorely tempted, listening to the immediate response of her innermost self. It was probably the right answer, if only because her first reaction was so quick and so positive. But was this the right time for her—for them? She cast her eyes around the room anxiously, as if some answer might be there for her. Not trusting herself to speak, she finally met Stoney's determined gaze.

"I mean it," Stoney repeated with conviction. "I want you to marry me."

"Oh, I know you do," she replied with a sound that was half a laugh of joy and half a sob of despair. If only things could be that easy. If only she could rush into his arms and say yes, and that would be that, all problems solved. But she knew it simply wasn't going to be that easy. There were too many problems to work out, too many outside factors to consider. She was torn in a million different directions, knowing that the only answer she wanted to make just wasn't possible for her at that time, that moment.

"Well?" Stoney prompted, his eager eyes searching her face, trying to read her expression.

Kiki sighed, trying to find the words that would

express her inner torment, words that would make him understand what she was experiencing. "I want to marry you, Stoney, I really do—"

"Then let's do it. Let's get married right away, right here if you want. Any place, any time, let's just do it." The questioning expression on his face had changed to one of ineffable joy, and Kiki could see that unless she stopped him right away, she was going to be in real trouble.

She held up a hand to silence him, to ward him off as he reached for her. If he held her in his arms right now, she would be lost. "I can't." She spoke the words in a quiet voice, but their effect was immediate and devastating.

"What do you mean, you *can't?*" Stoney's voice accused her. "Do you mean you *can't* or do you mean you *won't?*"

"I mean I can't—not right now, maybe not ever," Kiki replied as she struggled to hold back the tears that were threatening to betray her.

"But why? I love you, you love me—we were made for each other. You know that." He reached for her again, but she moved away.

"It's just not that simple for us," Kiki said, and her voice was sad. "We both have our work, so many other commitments. It seems to me the love we have between us would have a hard time surviving. And I can't give up my work. I simply can't be tied down, even to someone I love as much as I love you."

"I wouldn't tie you down," Stoney insisted. "It's not that I want a wife and kids and a house in the suburbs. You could have your work and I'd have mine."

"Right," Kiki replied firmly, "but if we both had our work, when would we find time to see each other?" She knew she had to be strong. "I don't think that now is the right time for this, Stoney."

Stoney's voice was soft and gentle as he asked his next question. "Are you saying that there might be some other time, the right time to ask this again?"

Kiki couldn't say no. Somewhere inside her there was still the hope that they could work it out. She didn't see how, but she still hoped for it. And who could say what might happen in the future; who could say where their lives might take them? She only knew that her life was taking her away from Stoney—taking her away that very night—and she was reluctant to have the departure be a final one. Do what's possible for you, she told herself, but keep hoping for the impossible. Keep hoping that somehow this can be worked out. "Yes, Stoney," she said finally, "some other time might be the right time. But this just isn't it. I have to finish packing and you have a show to do, remember?" She showed him her watch and the brief touch of his finger on her wrist was almost unbearably poignant.

"You're right." Stoney looked as if he couldn't believe the time had sped by so quickly. He leaned forward and brushed her lips with his, but Kiki refused to succumb to the emotions the brief touch aroused in her and she gently pushed him away. "All right," he shot back over his shoulder as he jumped out of bed. "This is not a one-time offer. I've got a lot more to say on this subject later." He stopped for a moment, looking as if he would like to say something more, but then, thinking better of it, he headed for the shower, leaving Kiki alone in the big bed.

What would he think of next? Kiki asked herself. Later! At the moment, she wasn't even sure there would *be* a later. Her last few hours in Nashville were passing all too quickly. This time tomorrow night she would be back in her loft in New York, missing him. A single tear rolled down her cheek, the only indication of the tension she had been under and the bargain she had struck with herself.

Now stop that, she told herself. Make the most of these hours you have left. Resolutely, she began putting on her makeup, listening to Stoney singing away in the shower. It should be a special night for Stoney and she resolved not to disappoint him. By the time they were both dressed and ready to go, she had managed to recover her good spirits, firmly pushing away all thoughts of her late flight.

Thirty minutes later, she and Stoney slipped in the back door of Ryman Auditorium, and both were giggling as they quickly slammed the door behind them.

"I thought we were goners for sure," Stoney said, leaning against the closed door, trying to catch his breath. Outside, a large crowd was already gathering, and Kiki and Stoney had been forced to go around the block and through a back door.

"What do you mean—we?" Kiki said with a laugh, delighted to find that she was actually enjoying herself. "It was you they were after, not me. I just thought I should keep you company. You needed some protection."

"And you were going to protect me?" Stoney said, looking down at her fondly, a smile on his face. He wore a black western shirt and close-fitting black pants. Kiki thought he had never been more appealing than he was at that moment.

"You bet," Kiki said, shrugging as if it were nothing. "I haven't told you about my black belt in karate?" she teased, feigning nonchalance.

Stoney burst into laughter as he put his arm around her shoulder. "I'm glad to know I was in such capable hands." Their eyes locked in a loving gaze. "You know, I—" Stoney's voice had been suddenly serious, and Kiki was relieved when Tully interrupted them. They'd had enough heart-to-heart talk for one day. And they were right back where they'd started.

"Okay, you two lovebirds. Let's get this show on the road." In spite of his casual attitude and light-hearted words, Kiki could tell that he was anything but calm.

"I think it's about time for me to join the audience. Just let me get a couple of good—" She had already started to take out her camera when Stoney interrupted her.

"She never gives up, does she?" Stoney said to Tully.

"We won't know how to act without a camera breathing down our necks," Tully agreed jovially, though it was obvious that he too dreaded her leave-taking.

"Oh, you guys are all impossible," Kiki said, not eager to get into another conversation on the subject of her departure. With a friendly wave in their direction, she started taking some close-ups of Ramsey and Ace. Photographing the group as they warmed up was always a little tricky. In spite of the inevitable clowning around, everyone was also very tense. This night was no exception. Seeing that Stoney was not completely engrossed in his work, Kiki quietly finished what she was doing and made her way out to the front where a standing-room-only crowd was eagerly awaiting Stoney Blue's appearance.

If Kiki had had any thoughts about sitting with the audience, she quickly brushed them aside—the large building was already packed with enthusiastic and loyal fans. And it was clear they were ready for the show to begin. A thrill of anticipation ran through her slender form, and she realized that she too was eager to hear Stoney sing.

When she slipped backstage again, Stoney and the band were ready to start. A stagehand was testing the microphones and another was making last-minute adjustments to the lights. Settling herself comfortably in a folding chair off to one side of the stage, Kiki decided that she'd taken enough pictures for a while. She was determined to watch at least part of the show, and she blew a kiss to Stoney as he looked over in her direction. He seemed to visibly relax when he saw that she was there.

Moments later, the curtain was drawn and the show began—Stoney sitting casually on the piano bench in a pose that had become his trademark. He started off slow and easy, and from the first notes, Kiki knew that they were all at their best. As they moved easily through the second and third songs, Kiki found that she was finally relaxing.

It's going to be all right, she said to herself. All those hours of rehearsing have paid off. They were ready for the big time! Kiki could tell by their thunderous applause that the audience agreed with her. Since she sensed that they had everything under control, Kiki began to feel a little restless. She knew Stoney would tease her if he knew, but she was determined to get some pictures from the back of the auditorium. Realizing that she would never get through the crowd, she grabbed her camera and hurried out the back door, hoping Stoney was too absorbed to notice her absence.

The streets were practically empty and Kiki had no trouble circling the building. Showing her press credentials to the usher, she made her way through the crowded lobby and managed to squeeze her way through until she found an opening at the back of the auditorium where she was able to take some pictures. She was so absorbed in her work that she was astonished when Stoney began his last song. She had completely lost track of the time. The crowd was insisting on an encore when Kiki reluctantly put away her camera and made her way back outside.

But it wasn't easy. Some of the stragglers who hadn't gotten seats were already running around the auditorium to the backstage door, obviously hoping to get a glimpse of Stoney when he left. By the time Kiki made her way to the narrow alley behind the theater, a large crowd had already gathered.

I should have known! she said to herself in exasperation. I don't know what I could have been thinking
of. Trudging back to the front of the theater, Kiki
waited for what seemed like an eternity while excited
fans poured out of the place. As soon as it was
possible, she made her way through the lobby to the
auditorium, thinking maybe she could get backstage
through the side door.

To her dismay, she saw that the stage was surrounded by thrilled fans, all trying to get Stoney's
autograph. Trying to decide what to do next, Kiki
made her way as close to the stage as possible,
hoping that Stoney would see her dilemma. She
glanced at her watch, realizing that time was rapidly
running out. If she didn't get to Stoney soon, she'd
have to take a taxi back to the hotel and go on to the
airport alone.

But Stoney was obviously enjoying his moment of
glory, and Kiki soon realized that at that minute she
was just another fan. She struggled to make her way
through the crowd surrounding Stoney, but progress
was slow. She could see him, smiling and grinning at
the crowd of women as he signed autographs for
them. Every now and then one of them would throw
her arms around him and Kiki noticed that Stoney
kissed a number of women. A pang went through
her as she remembered the taste, the feel of those
lips on hers only a few hours before. At the moment,
it seemed like there were simply too many women in
Stoney's life—and she, Kiki, was only part of the
crowd.

She kept waving frantically, hoping to at least have

a chance to signal Stoney that she was saying goodbye, but it seemed that he was only paying attention to the inner circle of the crowd. She called his name a few times with increasing urgency, but her cry was lost in the din of people struggling to get closer to him.

The romantic in Kiki somehow believed that if Stoney really loved her, he would somehow, with some sixth sense, know that she was trying to get close to him. But as it was, he seemed totally engrossed in what was going on around him. He didn't even seem to be looking around for her. Another glance at her watch showed that time was running out. She'd have to leave now if she wanted to make that plane and she knew she had to be on it.

Her eyes brimming with tears, Kiki hurried out to the street, determined to keep her composure. How clear it all was to her very suddenly! Stoney was in his element, that was plain to see. And she didn't fit in. Well, that's that, she told herself. She was just another face in the crowd, and she saw too clearly that they were painfully separated by the inevitable trappings of their careers. She feared that would always come between them as it had this evening. She had to face facts, hard as they were. Blinking back the tears that were threatening to overflow, she glanced at her watch as she headed down the street toward the hotel. She had just enough time to catch her plane. She would get her luggage from the hotel where she had checked it at the front desk and catch a taxi to the airport. She couldn't stand goodbyes anyway, and she and Stoney had already said all there was to say. It was time she started living her own life again. The lovemaking of that early evening was a bittersweet memory for her—it was the last time she and Stoney would be together for a long time—if not forever.

9

·················

Kiki glanced at her watch and groaned with frustration. Late again! It seemed that ever since she'd come home to New York, she was never able to get anywhere on time—as though she'd completely lost the knack of successfully hailing taxis and catching subways. Even though she'd been back for several weeks, it didn't seem that she was readjusting to life in the city at all well. To add to her frustration, it was beginning to rain. She held her portfolio over her head for protection, cursing the bulky camera case that hung from her shoulder, and braved the traffic to hail yet another taxi. This time, the cabbie took pity on her and stopped.

"Where to, lady?" he asked, and after Kiki had given him the address of the SoHo gallery, she sank back into the seat and sighed with relief. At least she knew she'd make it eventually, even though she'd be half an hour late.

She thought back to her morning meeting with Sid at the magazine. He had handed her the galleys of the issue with her photo-essay on Stoney Blue, due out on the stands in a few weeks, and congratulated her on a job well done. "It took a while, I know." He grinned at her. "But believe me, it was well worth it. Our readers will love it!"

Then, to her surprise, he pulled out a small, square, padded mailing envelope. "This came in the mail this morning. I thought that if anyone at the magazine would be interested in this, it would be you. After all, you were there when it was all happening."

Puzzled, Kiki opened it and pulled out a small 45 record in a plain white jacket. "It's a promotional copy of a song off Stoney's new album," Sid explained. "Just came this morning. They must have really rushed to have gotten a promo out this fast. It's called 'Stormy Serenade' according to the press release, and it's headed for the charts soon. I thought you might like to have it."

"Thanks," Kiki said without real conviction, though Sid didn't seem to pick up on it. Really, was there no escape from Stoney Blue? She'd spent days putting together the photo-essay, and now this! Was he destined to haunt her for the rest of her days? She tucked the record inside her portfolio and prepared to leave.

"And Kiki," Sid added, his eyes smiling behind the glasses he always wore. "You've been getting some great stuff—keep up the good work. Despite the slow start, I think this layout on Stoney is the best thing you've ever done. With that show coming up, good things are really going to start happening for you." His smile broadened as he teased her. "I just hope you remember all the little people who helped you along the way. . . ."

Kiki blushed and began to laugh in spite of herself. What would she have done without Sid? "You old joker," she teased back, "you just better be sure you show up at the opening. I want you there holding my hand every step of the way."

"Oh, I don't think you'll need anyone to hold your hand," Sid said airily. "But if you do, I'll start a waiting list. You've been away too long, lady. The men are going to be after you like bloodhounds when they find out you're back in town."

"Sure." Kiki laughed, walking out the door of his office. So far, the only men who had called had been on her list of what she laughingly referred to as "old reliables"—men who could be counted on for a good time but in whom she had no romantic interest whatsoever. Besides, Kiki just couldn't summon up interest in dating anyone—she was still too hung up on a handsome country-western singer with a rough beard and a gravelly voice. She wouldn't allow herself to think of his other attributes—like the way he looked first thing in the morning, the way his lips tasted when he kissed her.

Get hold of yourself, she admonished firmly as she waited for the elevator to take her down to the street. He's gone—he's out of your life—and you'll be lucky if you don't see him again ever. That man is trouble for you. You've got to keep your mind on your work now. You've got to get that show together and see where that leads. You've got to keep your mind where it belongs. Don't keep pining for something you can never have.

"We're here, lady," the cabbie announced, pulling over in front of Images Gallery and rousing Kiki from her reverie. Suddenly back in the present, she fumbled in her purse for cash and gathered up her things. Maybe her day was getting better, she reflected as she walked across the sidewalk to the gallery's front door. At least she'd been lucky enough to get a cabbie who didn't feel he had to make small talk.

"Ah, Kiki, you're here," came a soft, feminine voice from the back of the gallery. "I can't wait to see the new things you've brought."

Kiki smiled as she shook hands with Camilla Whitney, the owner of Images. During the time they had spent working on the show, the two women had discovered that they had a lot in common, and by now they were fast friends. It quickly went beyond a mere business relationship and soon Kiki had found herself confiding in Camilla about her whole affair with Stoney Blue. Surprisingly, it had been a relief to pour out the whole story to a sympathetic feminine ear. Camilla, realizing that it was difficult for Kiki to be constantly surrounded by reminders of the man, was nevertheless practical and direct in her response.

"What I think you need," she said calmly, "is to simply immerse yourself in it. You'll be surrounded with images of Stoney for a while, so that shouldn't be too hard to do. Then we'll do the show—which has a *lot* of important photographs in it besides the ones of Stoney. By the time the show is over, you'll be sick of seeing his face, metaphorically speaking, that is. Then you'll be immune to him, and you can go on to something—or someone—else."

Kiki had listened to the advice and tried to follow it, but it just didn't seem to be working. The more she looked at the photographs she'd taken of Stoney, the more she longed to see that familiar face in person. The more she looked at the gorgeous pictures of the Texas countryside, the more she longed to be back there with him. There didn't seem to be any therapy, any escape from the aching sense of loss which filled her days. And even though she knew Camilla's advice had seemed to make a certain amount of sense, she just didn't know if she'd ever get over the love she felt for Stoney. It was still there.

The two women spent an hour looking at the photos Kiki had brought with her. "Oh, these are great," Camilla exclaimed, closing the portfolio at last. "Leave them with me and I'll have them ready to hang for the show. But what's this?" She was looking at the manila envelope containing Stoney's record. It had been underneath the photographs in the portfolio, and Kiki had been attempting to forget all about it.

"Just another reminder of Stoney," Kiki smiled ruefully. "A promotional 45 of a new song came to the magazine today, and Sid thought that I'd like to have it. I haven't told him anything about how I felt about Stoney, so I decided that the best thing to do was simply to take it and leave."

"Perfect!" Camilla said firmly. "After you've heard it I'll tape it. It's the perfect music for the

162

opening of the show—the final touch for our Texas theme. This will be an opening no one will ever forget, I promise you that."

At the dismayed look on Kiki's face, Camilla became even more determined. "Look, Kiki, you're never going to get over this if you just keep moping around. So, at the opening, we'll have the pictures, we'll have the music. It will be a great success, and then we'll go out and have dinner at a fancy restaurant and celebrate the end of Stoney Blue— and the beginning of something else. Then you can get to work on getting enough stuff together to do your next show here."

"My next show?" Kiki asked, surprised and delighted. She had known Camilla liked her work, but she hadn't realized just how much.

"Right!" Camilla declared. "I'll give you about six months. In the meantime, I'd like to start handling your work on a more or less permanent basis. As it is, I'm sure we'll sell most of it at the show, and you'll simply have to hit the streets and produce some more great pictures." She smiled at Kiki's surprise. "My friend, you simply don't realize how good your work really is, do you?"

"I guess not," Kiki admitted softly. "But I'm glad you think so. It's just that right now I can't imagine what I'll be doing next—subjects, locations, nothing seems to spring to mind."

Camilla leaned over and took Kiki's hand in both of hers. "Kiki, you can work anywhere, don't you know that? You have the artist's eye. Why, you could take a photo of a cantaloupe and it would probably be wonderful!"

Soon they were both laughing at the ridiculous suggestion. "Well, at least then I wouldn't have a broken heart," Kiki said. "If the cantaloupe failed to cooperate, I could just go out and buy a new one."

Kiki gave the new photographs to Camilla and packed up her portfolio, preparing to leave. "Well, thanks," she said finally, giving Camilla a warm hug. "This has done me a world of good. You always do. And I can't wait until the opening. It will probably be the most exciting night of my life."

"Oh, I doubt that," Camilla said wryly. "Unless I miss my guess, you have a lot more openings ahead of you. I just hope that they'll all be right here," she said, gesturing to the spacious gallery.

"I hope so, too," Kiki said warmly. "I can't tell you what it means to me to have you for a friend."

"Oh, get out of here before we both get ridiculously sentimental." Camilla laughed. "Get out of here and get to work."

Kiki walked out to the street, noticing that the day seemed suddenly brighter. She even got a taxi on her first try, and headed back to the loft. All her roommates were out of town on assignment, and, for once, she found herself actually looking forward to the solitude. Maybe, with Camilla's help, she really was getting over Stoney. Maybe.

Back in the loft, she dumped her camera and portfolio on the desk in the workspace that she shared with her roommates. Reveling in the unaccustomed silence, she walked through to the bathroom and ran a hot bath for herself, tossing in liberal amounts of scented bath salts. Thinking that she would enjoy having this time to luxuriate in the tub, she went to the kitchen and poured herself a glass of wine, picked up a bestseller she had been meaning to read for weeks and, almost as an afterthought, went to the stereo and put on Stoney's record.

I know I'm going to regret this, she said to herself, but it's something I've just got to do. I know I'm going to hear it sooner or later anyway. Taking a sip of her wine, she retreated to the bathroom, where she quickly stripped and lowered her tired body into the warm, scented water. She tried to read the book, but after a few pages she gave up, lay back in the water and surrendered to the sound of Stoney's voice, which seemed to fill the entire loft.

It's no use, she told herself. I simply can't get him out of my system. She laughed as she remembered their day in the recording studio, knowing just how much work it took to get every song just right, remembering Stoney's quick humor with longing, even summoning up fondness for his occasional irritable moments. The music had been worth every minute of effort though, for the song was as perfect as a song can be, and hearing it brought tears to Kiki's eyes.

She thought back to that evening in the Warwick Hotel in Houston, when Stoney sat there and played the melody for her, remembering that that was the first time anyone had ever sung or played just for her. Determined not to give in to the tears that threatened to overflow, Kiki tried to talk herself out of being depressed.

It's just no good, she told herself firmly, it never would have worked out. He's got his life and I've got mine. Besides, if he really cared he would have called—sent a postcard—something. Sid would have given him my phone number, if he'd been interested, that is.

You fool! said a small voice in the back of her mind. *He asked you to marry him. What more do you want? You're the one who said you couldn't and wouldn't be tied down. He asked. You just turned him down. You have only yourself to blame.*

Suddenly her whole life seemed to be meaningless. So what if she was having a show at Images? So what if she had a life and friends in New York? Suddenly it didn't seem to matter. Ever since she'd been back in New York that life hadn't seemed worth living. If it hadn't been for Camilla's friendship and constant encouragement, she doubted if she'd even be going through with the show. All that mattered was a cowboy's smile. All that really seemed important was going back to Texas to find him again.

I could do that, Kiki said to herself excitedly. I could just show up on his doorstep and tell him I've changed my mind. No, I couldn't, she thought despondently, sinking back into the rapidly cooling water. I don't even know where he is. He's on tour. He could be in some little honky-tonk in Georgia by now, for all I know. I may never catch up with him again. Besides, he might not be so glad to see me. She frowned, remembering the crowd of adoring fans surrounding Stoney on the stage after his show in Nashville.

I bet he's found someone else by now, she said to herself. He looked too happy that night. And if he'd noticed I was gone, if he'd been sorry not to have said goodbye, he would have done something about it. He would have found *me* somehow—I just know he would.

Finally, no longer able to make sense of her muddled emotions, she allowed the tears to course down her face. In the living room, the stereo needle swung off the record, hesitated a second, then swung back. The strains of "Stormy Serenade" echoed through the vast white space, and so did the sobs of the woman who was convinced she had lost the singer forever.

10

⬥⬥⬥⬥⬥⬥⬥⬥⬥⬥

No, you're right, Sid," Kiki admitted, unable to meet the glance of her friend. "He wasn't just another subject, another assignment. He was much more than that. But how did you know?" The woeful look on her face changed to one of mild suspicion as she looked up at Sid.

"C'mon, Kiki. I'd have to be blind not to know. You haven't been the same since you came back. You hardly ever smile these days, much less laugh. And I've never seen you so obsessed with a batch of photographs. That's not like you—usually you're ready to finish up and move on to the next thing." Sid, sitting with his feet propped up on his desk, thoughtfully studied Kiki's face as he twirled a pencil between thumb and forefinger.

Kiki was silent for a moment, staring out the

window. "I didn't realize it was that obvious," she finally said, still looking out at the view. The New York City skyline no longer thrilled her heart and mind. Everything about the big city threatened to make her even more nostalgic for the wide-open Texas spaces.

"Well, it is, and I'm glad you finally admitted it. I hated to confront you with my suspicions, but after all, I'm one of your oldest friends and I've been concerned about you. And as your friend, I have to tell you that I think you're being pigheaded not to call and invite him to your opening tonight. If you called him right now, he'd still have time to catch a plane and get here in time to help us uncork the champagne." Sid sat up suddenly, picked up the phone receiver and held it out to Kiki.

"No, Sid. And that's my final word." Kiki hoped she sounded more determined than she actually felt at that moment. If the truth were to be told, the idea of calling Stoney and inviting him to the opening was very tempting—and had been for quite some time. But she was afraid he would turn her down flat and Kiki wasn't sure she could handle the rejection. She took the phone receiver from Sid and carefully but firmly replaced it. "He knows when the opening is. I told him before I left. If he cared, *he* would have called *me* by now. I'm not as hard to find as he is."

"That's the most stubborn thing I've heard you say yet, and you've pulled some lulus. Talk about cutting off your nose to spite your face! You're miserable without the guy, but you're just too hard-headed to do anything about it."

"Oh, Sid, I don't mean to be stubborn, but I've been here for a month, an entire month, without a single word from Stoney."

Sid's face darkened. "Well, I don't know what you expect after you ran out on him without even saying goodbye."

"How did you know about that?" Kiki demanded.

Sid looked as though he were sorry he'd mentioned it. "His manager called the next morning to be sure you'd gotten back safely. It sounds like they were all a little worried about you. And that's not like you either, Kiki." His expression was filled with concern.

"I know. I don't know what I could have been thinking of. We were both so upset that day. Neither one of us could do anything right. Oh, what a mess!" Kiki said forlornly, her gaze returning to the view from the window.

"I've never known you to give up so easily," Sid commented, shaking his head in disbelief.

"Well, there's a first time for everything, Sid," Kiki retorted, turning back to him with a determined look on her face. "Enough of this nonsense. I've got to get going. If I don't hurry, I'll be late for my interview with Carol Covington."

"Is that today?" Sid asked.

"You know it's today. I reminded you this morning," Kiki said with a touch of impatience. "We're having lunch at Tavern on the Green. And it's almost one o'clock now, so I'll have to hurry. I'm really anxious to hear what she thinks of the show. Camilla gave her a special preview last night so she could get started on the article." Kiki paused at the door and turned to add, "Don't worry about me, Sid. I can take care of myself." Before he had a chance to reply, she breezed out of the office.

Quickly leaving the building, she grabbed a taxi to Tavern on the Green, hoping that she wouldn't be too late. She had been surprised when Carol Covington, the prestigious critic from *PhotoArt*, had called and asked her to lunch, but she had quickly agreed. An article in *PhotoArt* was the first big step toward being recognized as an artist as well as a journalist. Kiki knew that she should be elated, but she was unable to shake the melancholy which enveloped her like a cloud. The show would open that night; important people were beginning to take an interest in her work—what more could she want?

What a question! she said to herself as she entered the restaurant. What a question! And she knew the answer all too well, though she didn't want to admit it to herself. The only thing she could want was for Stoney to call or come—to be together one more time.

Fortunately, lunch with Carol Covington seemed to be just the thing for lifting Kiki out of her depression. She was pleased at the perceptiveness of the critic's questions as well as her lavish praise. Leaving the restaurant several hours later, Kiki felt almost excited about the coming evening. She knew that if Carol Covington liked her work and wrote the article she had outlined for Kiki over lunch, her career as an independent photographer was well on its way. Now if only she could get through the opening without succumbing to thoughts of Stoney. If only she could carry this off!

Stepping out of the cab and paying the driver, Kiki stood for a second, surveying the building in which she lived. When she had first moved into the loft with her friends, she had thought it was wonderful—so chic, so trendy—just the sort of space an artist craved. Now, knowing that her roommates were out of town and that she would be alone, it suddenly seemed cold and empty and strangely forbidding. Not at all like Stoney's ranch, which was truly a home.

Reminding herself that this was her big night, she resolved to recapture her festive mood. Entering the building, she found a bottle of champagne and a beautiful vase of flowers on her doorstep. In spite of herself, she had to fight back the rising hope that one or both of them would be from Stoney—maybe he had remembered after all. She opened the door and carried them into the loft, placing her burdens carefully on the long glass table in the dining room. The card on the champagne was written in Camilla's strong clear handwriting—"Just an inkling of things to come. Thought you might like to start celebrating early." Kiki smiled at the thoughtfulness of the gallery owner, and took the bottle to the refrigerator. Now for the flowers. The card was attached to one of the yellow roses in the arrangement, and Kiki couldn't keep from thinking of the song "The Yellow Rose of Texas," hoping that Stoney was behind this. But when she opened the envelope, the message was from Sid. "It should have been orchids." Kiki laughed despite her disappointment. She was grateful for the silent support she knew was behind the gesture. She was lucky in her boss, that was for sure.

Glancing at her watch, Kiki realized that she was going to have to hurry to get ready, and she was grateful that she wasn't going to have a lot of time to think about the rapidly approaching opening.

After a quick shower, Kiki went into her bedroom to dress, glad that she had already chosen her outfit for that evening. She slipped into an elegant black cowboy shirt, trimmed with silver cord, a trim pair of designer jeans, cinching the narrow waist with a western belt with beaten silver tips and buckle, and pulled on a pair of comfortable leather boots. If the opening had a western theme, she certainly looked the part. And she felt comfortable. She felt good about the way she looked and what was going to happen.

As well she should, she scolded herself. She'd worked hard for this success and she was going to enjoy it, even if it killed her. She wasn't going to let some starry-eyed, deep-voiced country singer who wouldn't even be there spoil it for her. She went to the kitchen and retrieved the bottle of champagne, thinking that she deserved a glass while she waited for the taxi. She sipped at the bubbly liquid and felt excitement rise within her, lifting her spirits for the next moment. Tonight was going to be a good night, she could feel it. Good things were going to happen for her. The tide was turning.

When she heard the taxi honk outside, she got her things together, locked the door with her customary caution and bounded down the stairs, champagne glass still in hand. Settling herself in the back seat, she laughed as she gave the address to the cab driver, conscious that he was giving her questioning looks for the champagne glass in her hand.

When Kiki saw the crowd of people already waiting inside the gallery, she was tempted to tell the cab driver to take her home. Instead, she asked him to circle the block a few times to give her a chance to collect her thoughts. He looked at her quizzically, but did as she asked. Finally, Kiki decided it was now or never—after all, they had come to see her as well as her photographs, and she knew it would be absolutely awful if she were late for her own opening.

Paying the driver, Kiki crossed the sidewalk to the door of the gallery, grateful that she could already glimpse a few familiar faces from the offices of *Lifestyle*. Sid greeted her at the door with a bear hug.

"It's marvelous, Kiki, absolutely marvelous. Everyone loves the show. Why didn't you show me some of the other photographs you took while you were on the road with Stoney? All *I* got to see were pictures of Stoney and the band. Now those were good enough, but some of these others are just fantastic!" He smiled down at her, obviously pleased with her success.

"Oh, Sid." Kiki laughed. "You're a one-man fan club, you know that? I didn't show you the others because they weren't part of the assignment and because I wasn't sure you'd like them. They aren't exactly photo-journalism, are they?"

"No, they're not, Kiki. They're much, much more. I can't imagine why you worried about showing them to me. They're great, but then I always knew you could do it."

Sid would have gone on and on if the two of them hadn't been interrupted by Camilla Whitney. "Kiki, where have you been? Everyone's wild about the work—and a good bit of it's been sold already. Carol Covington just bought one of your best, but of course, that's only to be expected. Don't you just *love* it?" She gestured to the crowd milling around the gallery.

For the first time, Kiki was really able to look around and see what was going on. At least sixty or seventy people were walking around the gallery, all of them studying her work, and each other, with total fascination. But that wasn't what caught Kiki's attention. Everywhere she looked, she seemed to see Stoney's face staring back at her from the gallery walls. It seemed to her, for a moment at least, that she had taken photographs only of him, nothing else. As Camilla had promised, she had taped Stoney's new song and now the familiar strains of "Stormy Serenade" filled the rooms. Kiki was overwhelmed with the sense of his presence—his face, his voice—and for a moment she was sorry that she hadn't taken Sid's advice and called him that morning.

Stop that right now, she told herself firmly. This is your night. You just forget about that man and enjoy yourself. This is a once-in-a-lifetime evening. And for a while, Kiki almost succeeded. She greeted old friends and Camilla introduced her to new ones— Kiki thought she had never met so many people in one evening. She struggled to match names with faces, wishing for a moment that she had her camera so she could capture some of this on film.

Sid must have read her thoughts, for he quickly came to her side, pointing out another photographer from the magazine who was unobtrusively taking lots of pictures of the crowd. "Knew it wouldn't be appropriate for you to be taking pictures tonight, so I thought I'd get someone from the magazine to take care of that for you. It would be terribly ironic if you of all people didn't have any pictures of a special evening like this."

Kiki smiled at him gratefully, thinking that it was just like Sid to have thought of everything. "Thanks," she said softly, "you know that means a lot to me."

"Say nothing of it," Sid said airly. "Besides, you know me. I always have an ulterior motive. *Lifestyle* might be doing a spread on you before you know it."

"Don't you dare." Kiki grinned, fearing that the threat was not an idle one. Sid smiled and turned back to the crowd, obviously enjoying himself a little at her expense.

Kiki continued to enjoy the evening in spite of one bad moment when an attractive woman who'd been admiring a photograph of Stoney turned to her with excitement in her eyes. "You mean you actually met Stoney Blue?" she asked.

"Why, yes," Kiki said, and turned to go. For a fleeting moment, she thought bitterly to herself that the woman was much too old to be so starstruck, but Kiki was determined to be cordial. However, the woman was not to be sidestepped so easily. "And isn't that his new song playing in the background?"

"Yes," Kiki admitted. "We got a promotional copy at the magazine, and Camilla taped it for the opening. She wanted a Texas theme for the evening, and the music seemed to be a nice touch." Nice for everyone but her, she thought to herself, remembering with a pang her idyllic time with Stoney in Nashville. No matter what she did, she seemed unable to escape the memories with which the evening surrounded her.

"Well, what was he really like?" the woman demanded. "I mean really?"

Kiki decided that the best way to handle the situation was to be self-deprecating. "Actually, he seemed like a pretty nice guy. But you have to remember that I've photographed lots of people, many of them famous people, for the magazine. He was no more or less special than any of my other subjects."

The woman arched an eyebrow in Kiki's direction, her expression one of obvious disbelief. "For a photographer, you certainly seem to have poor eyesight when it comes to some things. Besides, there's a rumor going around that he might actually be coming tonight. Is there any truth to that?"

"I'm sure there isn't," Kiki said firmly, wondering how such a strange story could have been circulated. If Stoney actually were going to come, she was sure she would have known. After all, it was her opening. She decided to ask Camilla if she knew how such a story could have gotten around, and she gave the woman a cordial good evening and went in search of the gallery owner.

She found Camilla in the gallery office marking sales on a long sheet of paper. Looking up and seeing Kiki in the doorway, Camilla gave her friend a brilliant smile and told her to have a seat, going behind her to close the door.

"Well, how does it feel to be a success?" She grinned wickedly. "You couldn't have found me at a better time. I've been totaling the receipts. Things are selling very well. We've made ourselves a tidy little sum this evening, I'll have you know."

"You're kidding." Kiki was genuinely astonished. "You mean people are actually buying my photographs?"

"Why not?" Camilla demanded. "If I hadn't thought your photos were fantastic I wouldn't have taken you on. I have high hopes for our future working relationship, you know. I'm not in the art business for my health, after all."

Kiki had to laugh at her friend's forthright honesty, and she was glad that they were going to be working together. But suddenly she remembered why she had been looking for Camilla in the first place. "Listen," she began, not wanting to sound silly, but feeling that she had to ask, "there's a woman out there who says there's a rumor going around that—" She and Camilla were both suddenly startled by the sound of wholehearted applause from the gallery.

"I guess I'd better get out there and see what's going on," Camilla said, rising quickly and going to the door, a strange smile on her face.

"I'll come too," Kiki said quickly, feeling a surge of curiosity as well as an unexpected sense of foreboding. Besides, she knew that she really should get back to the guests. She didn't want anyone to know how hard this evening really was for her and she was determined to look as if she were enjoying herself every minute.

It was hard to tell what was going on when the two women went out of the office, for the scene that greeted them was one of absolute pandemonium. The back of the gallery was virtually empty, and the crowd of people had surged toward the front door, surrounding the late arrival. Kiki glanced at Camilla, a question in her eyes, but she was only rewarded with the same knowing smile she had noticed in Camilla's office.

Through the crush of people, Kiki could hear Sid saying "I think she's in the back" to someone and she wondered if he were talking about her. Then suddenly, it seemed as if the crowd were parting to make way for someone, and she could see a tall familiar figure walking toward her through the sea of people. The minute Kiki recognized him, she had an impulse to flee, to leave, to go anywhere she could to get away from him, but her eyes met his and she knew there was no escaping.

Praying that her voice didn't betray her tumultuous feelings, she said softly, "Hello, cowboy."

"Hello, gorgeous." Stoney was beside her now, his eyes searching hers as they had that first night so long ago in the Astrodome when they had discovered each other in the crowd.

Kiki felt her heart beat a little faster at his nearness but she held back momentarily, not at all certain what to do next. After all, it had been a long time. Maybe he had changed. Maybe he was in New York on other business. Maybe he had just happened by, she thought, knowing immediately how ridiculous that was.

"That's some vanishing act you've got," Stoney said softly, his eyes never leaving her face. He was beside her, his hand-tailored western-cut suit a perfect complement to his lean muscular form.

Kiki cringed at the memory of her leaving without saying goodbye, but she kept her voice steady as she retorted, "It's not much better than your mob scene."

Without any apparent concern for the crowd of people watching them, he continued in the same deep voice she had missed during the last month. "I've missed you." And his piercing blue eyes confirmed his words.

Kiki felt his voice and eyes caress her as surely as if he had touched her, and, forgetting for the moment where she was, she responded with her whole heart. "Oh, I've missed you too, Stoney, I really have." She stood on tiptoe to receive his kiss, not at all aware of the satisfied glances Sid and Camilla were exchanging, knowing only that she was back in Stoney's arms where she belonged.

His warm mouth came down on hers in that kiss she remembered so well, and she knew she was lost to the flurry of sensations that this man always aroused in her. Oblivious to the crowd of people around them, the two of them were lost in their warm embrace, renewing the passion which existed between them as if they had never missed a moment. Finally, drawing back from Stoney's welcome embrace, Kiki looked around her and realized that the crowd in the gallery was watching them with approval, for as soon as they broke apart, the crowd erupted into spontaneous applause.

Kiki was momentarily embarrassed at having been brought back so suddenly into the present, but she quickly recovered, especially after seeing the expressions on the faces of Camilla and Sid. Stoney too had turned to face the crowd, keeping one strong arm about her waist. Kiki was grateful for the support, the tangible reminder that he was indeed present in the flesh.

"Glad you could make it," Sid said jovially, stepping up to shake hands with Stoney.

"Me too," Stoney said, laughing down in Kiki's direction. "Don't you think it worked? Don't you think she was truly surprised?"

Kiki sputtered with exasperation at this open admission of their conspiracy. "You mean you had this all planned?" she demanded, casting a frustrated look in Sid's direction.

"Well." Sid grinned. "It would have been a whole lot easier if you'd just picked up the phone this morning the way I asked you to. Stoney had sworn me to secrecy, but when I saw how depressed you were this morning it was all I could do to keep from telling you. If you'd just called him, well, it would have been a lot easier. But since you were being so stubborn and pigheaded, the surprise served you right."

"I hadn't forgotten the date," Stoney said, "but I was afraid you'd tell me not to come if I asked you. The way you left me high and dry I thought maybe you didn't ever want to see me again. But I knew I had to see you again, so when I called Sid to tell him I was coming, I made him promise not to tell you. I said I wanted it to be a surprise."

"And surprise me you did." Kiki laughed, unable to be angry with Stoney or Sid or Camilla, who was also looking on with laughter. "And a lovely surprise it is." She looked up at Stoney's dear face and relished the welcome sight. Even if she had been too stubborn to ask him to come herself, she knew it was the answer to her dreams. It was worth anything just to taste his kiss, feel his arms around her one more time.

Fortunately, the crowd in the gallery had gotten back to the party, as if deciding by some tacit agreement to give Kiki and Stoney some privacy. Kiki noted with gratitude that things seemed to be winding down somewhat, but she couldn't help wondering what would happen next.

"This looks like a first-class show you've got here," Stoney said, putting his arm around her shoulders. They walked over to look at the photographs.

"Just a little something I threw together," Kiki said with a grin.

"Yeah, I bet," Stoney countered, his blue eyes full of admiration.

"Come on, let me give you the grand tour," Kiki said enthusiastically. "I think you'll recognize some of the faces." For the next thirty minutes, Stoney and Kiki moved around the gallery, carefully studying the photographs.

"They're wonderful," Stoney said, truly impressed. "And after all that talk about being too involved with the subject. I don't think your professional eye is lacking anything," he said softly, looking down at her tenderly.

"Well," she admitted slowly, "maybe love's not blind after all."

"I'd say that's a real possibility," Stoney drawled as he put his arms around her tiny waist and drew her closer. "Do you have any plans for later?"

Kiki mulled his question over thoughtfully, as if she had to remember. "Nothing special, come to think of it." The twinkle in her eye gave her away. "You got any ideas?"

"Well, as a matter of fact," Stoney said, "I've been doing some thinking about that very thing." Bending low to whisper in her ear, he added, "Why don't we start out at your place? After all, you've seen my home. Now I think it's my turn."

A few moments later, Kiki followed Stoney into the back of the waiting limousine. "Remember?" he teased her gently. "Remember the day I told you that if I had my way I'd make sure that life was always full of lovely surprises for you?"

"I do, indeed." Kiki smiled, savoring the memory with pleasure. "I do indeed."

Outside her building, Stoney dismissed the limousine with instructions to call again the next morning. Certainly sure of himself, that man is, Kiki thought to herself, but she found that she didn't really care. She was just glad to have him with her again.

As they entered the doorway of the loft, Stoney

swung her up in his arms and carried her over the threshold ceremoniously. "I hope to be doing this again soon," he whispered in her ear. "I hope to be doing this again really soon—whether it's here or in Texas, anywhere you say, Kiki. I know that we can work it out."

Kiki flushed with pleasure, remembering the last time he had asked her to marry him. This time there was no question as to her answer—she didn't ever want to go through what she had this past month without Stoney—but she knew that they still had a few things to work out.

"I know we can too," she admitted after Stoney had gently placed her back on her feet. He followed her into the kitchen, where she removed the bottle of champagne she had opened earlier and poured him a glass. "I've been doing some thinking, you know."

"Me too," he said quickly. "You know that I'm on the road a lot, but people seem to have a lot of luck these days with commuter marriages. As long as we can plan our time together, I don't see any reason why we can't work it out. You know I love you."

"And I love you too," she said quickly, wanting to speak before her courage failed her. "I don't see any reason why it shouldn't work out. Camilla said that I can work anywhere, and that she'd sell my work for me in the future. And I don't like this place anymore." She gestured to the gleaming kitchen with its elaborate high-tech furnishings. "I don't mean just the kitchen," she added, seeing his quizzical glance.

"I mean New York—it's so cold and unfriendly. Ever since I met you I realized how much I miss Texas. I want to go home—I want to go home with you, Stoney."

Stoney swooped down and gathered her in his arms, letting out a whoop of pure joy. "Those are the best words I've heard all day," he said. "Let me take you home to Texas, Kiki. I want to. Just as soon as you're ready."

Kiki gave herself up to the pleasure of his embrace, knowing that it was the first of many to come. She couldn't believe she had ever doubted that she was important to Stoney; she couldn't believe that it had been so easy to sort things out. Oh, there would be problems ahead. But somehow nothing seemed impossible now that they were together again.

As if in a single thought for what would happen next, both of them placed their champagne glasses on the kitchen counter, and Kiki led Stoney to her bedroom, grateful for the first time since she had come to New York that her roommates were out of town. As he followed her down the hall, Stoney began to hum in a low voice—the voice she remembered and loved so well—the song he had written just for her: "Stormy Serenade." Now the song held no pain for her, only the promise of their future.

They undressed each other gently, savoring the renewed pleasure of their reunion after the long separation. Stoney caressed each part of her with tenderness, as if he couldn't believe that she was really with him again. For her part, Kiki reexplored the familiar joys of Stoney's body, as if she too couldn't believe that the long dark days of their being apart were over. Slowly, with infinite passion and joy, they were reunited in love, the stormy serenade of their early relationship ending in a rainbow of pleasure they would share—forever.

Silhouette Desire
15-Day Trial Offer

A new romance series
that explores
contemporary relationships
in exciting detail

Six Silhouette Desire romances, free for 15 days!
We'll send you six new Silhouette Desire romances
to look over for 15 days, absolutely free! If you decide
not to keep the books, return them and owe nothing.

Six books a month, free home delivery. If you like
Silhouette Desire romances as much as we think you
will, keep them and return your payment with the
invoice. Then we will send you six new books every
month to preview, just as soon as they are published.
You pay only for the books you decide to keep, and
you never pay postage and handling.

YOU'LL BE SWEPT AWAY
WITH SILHOUETTE DESIRE

$1.75 each

Silhouette Desire

- 50 ☐ FRIENDS AND LOVERS
  Palmer
- 51 ☐ SHADOW OF THE
  MOUNTAIN Lind
- 52 ☐ EMBERS OF THE SUN
  Morgan
- 53 ☐ WINTER LADY Joyce
- 54 ☐ IF EVER YOU NEED ME
  Fulford
- 55 ☐ TO TAME THE HUNTER
  James
- 56 ☐ FLIP SIDE OF YESTERDAY
  Douglass
- 57 ☐ NO PLACE FOR A WOMAN
  Michelle
- 58 ☐ ONE NIGHT'S DECEPTION
  Mallory
- 59 ☐ TIME STANDS STILL
  Powers
- 60 ☐ BETWEEN THE LINES
  Dennis
- 61 ☐ ALL THE NIGHT LONG
  Simms
- 62 ☐ PASSIONATE SILENCE
  Monet
- 63 ☐ SHARE YOUR
  TOMORROWS Dee
- 64 ☐ SONATINA
  Milan

- 65 ☐ RECKLESS VENTURE
  Allison
- 66 ☐ THE FIERCE GENTLENESS
  Langtry
- 67 ☐ GAMEMASTER
  James
- 68 ☐ SHADOW OF YESTERDAY
  Browning
- 69 ☐ PASSION'S PORTRAIT
  Carey
- 70 ☐ DINNER FOR TWO
  Victor
- 71 ☐ MAN OF THE HOUSE
  Joyce
- 72 ☐ NOBODY'S BABY
  Hart
- 73 ☐ A KISS REMEMBERED
  St. Claire
- 74 ☐ BEYOND FANTASY
  Douglass
- 75 ☐ CHASE THE CLOUDS
  McKenna
- 76 ☐ STORMY SERENADE
  Michelle
- 77 ☐ SUMMER THUNDER
  Lowell
- 78 ☐ BLUEPRINT FOR RAPTURE
  Barber

SILHOUETTE DESIRE, Department SD/6
1230 Avenue of the Americas
New York, NY 10020

Please send me the books I have checked above. I am enclosing $_____
(please add 50¢ to cover postage and handling. NYS and NYC residents please add
appropriate sales tax.) Send check or money order—no cash or C.O.D.'s please.
Allow six weeks for delivery.

NAME _____

ADDRESS _____

CITY _____ STATE/ZIP _____

READERS' COMMENTS ON SILHOUETTE DESIRES

"Thank you for Silhouette Desires. They are the best thing that has happened to the bookshelves in a long time."

—V.W.*, Knoxville, TN

"Silhouette Desires—wonderful, fantastic—the best romance around."

—H.T.*, Margate, N.J.

"As a writer as well as a reader of romantic fiction, I found DESIREs most refreshingly realistic—and definitely as magical as the love captured on their pages."

—C.M.*, Silver Lake, N.Y.

*names available on request